Enter The Pistollera
TALES OF THE PURPLE PISTOLLERA I

JASIAH WITKOFSKY

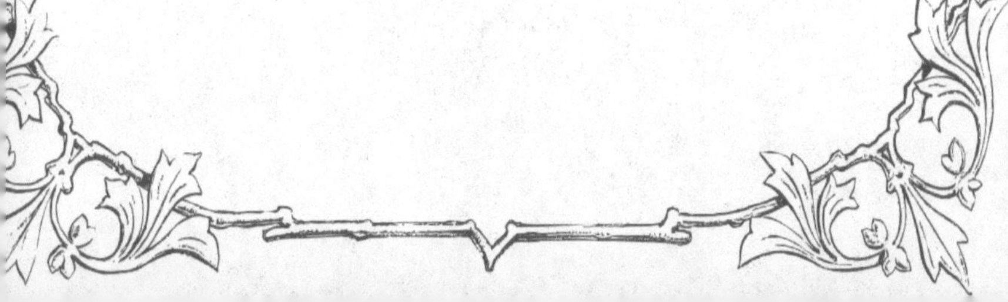

Nordic Press
Kindlyckevägen 13
590 43 Rimforsa
Copyright 2023 by Jasiah Witkofsky
Back plate by Dan Gregor.
Rose Xylona Ayala
Digital Colorizations of the back cover.
Interior art by siblings; Gordo, JenJen, and JaDa.
Proofreads, story assistance, and character creations
from Chris Hall and Mike Kieran.
Translations by Julia Bernadini and Joesph Douville.
Photography by Mike Meals (Punk Paparazzi).
Model and Muse by the Lovely Lydia Lesnyakov.
Cover by C. Marry Hultman
Formatting and setting by C. Marry Hultman
Publisher enquiries
www.nordicpresspublishing.com

Acknowledgements

Stacy Morrighan McIntosh for publishing the first Pistollera story.
And David Green with Christopher Marry Hultman and the entire crew of Nordic Press for giving a nobody a chance.

"Rascals, would you live forever?"
--Frederick II the Great

CONTENTS

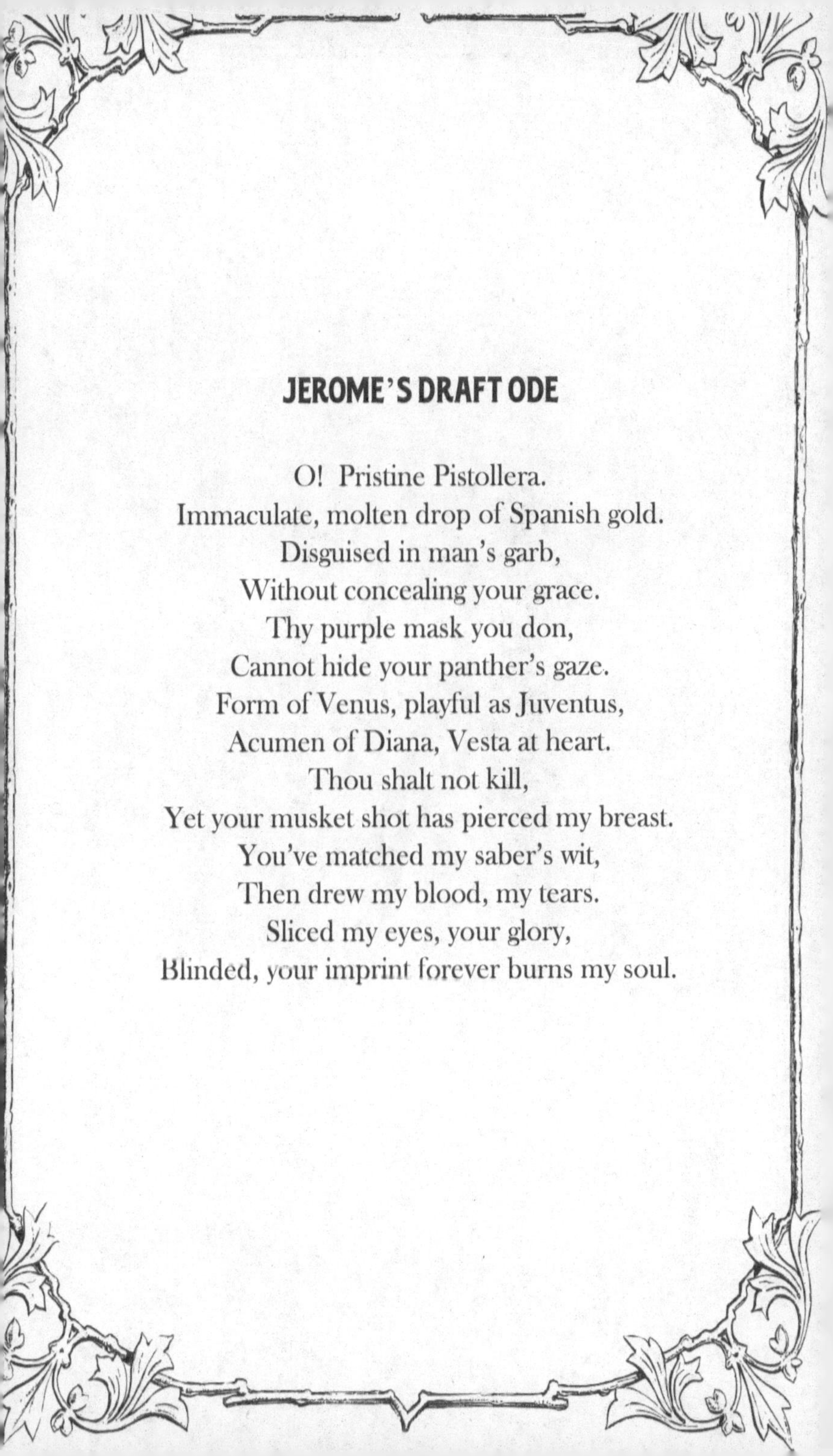

JEROME'S DRAFT ODE

O! Pristine Pistollera.
Immaculate, molten drop of Spanish gold.
Disguised in man's garb,
Without concealing your grace.
Thy purple mask you don,
Cannot hide your panther's gaze.
Form of Venus, playful as Juventus,
Acumen of Diana, Vesta at heart.
Thou shalt not kill,
Yet your musket shot has pierced my breast.
You've matched my saber's wit,
Then drew my blood, my tears.
Sliced my eyes, your glory,
Blinded, your imprint forever burns my soul.

ENTRA NELLA PISTOLLERA
A JOYFUL VENTURE

This is the tale of an orphan girl from the principality of Catalonia, during that flamboyant era known as the Baroque, a time of nobility, artists, explorers, and pirates, nestled between the innovative Renaissance and the calculating period of the Enlightenment. Raised in a nunnery within the municipality of Barcelona, the young Dolores Llorenc learned her letters from Scripture, and obfuscation avoiding the punitive lashings of mentors in habits. At the dawning of womanhood, the diminutive maiden found a way to escape the cloister, spending the nights roaming the streets and docksides of Catalonia's majestic capital, the City of Counts.

It was during these moonlit sojourns that Dolores became aware of the seedier side of humanity. The haggling, brawls, seductions, thefts, and briberies did not pass unnoticed before the golden-brown eyes of the innocent. This led to a crisis of belief, a dichotomy between the ordered sanctity revealed by the sun, and the dirty underbelly concealed by the darkness.

The lure of the night was too enticing for the orphan, too enthralling to contain in one miniscule being, so she invited from amongst her sheltered peers a handful of her closest confidants to temporarily break free from the confines of the nunnery. The infinitude of the outside world held the ability to bewitch all, and the girls took to the open air, and their own proclivities towards temptation. One became fond of the intoxication of the vine, another enamored by strapping young lads, one longed to dance, but Dolores's inclination was to watch and learn from the gambler, the sneak, and the sailor. Men of skill, of action, who lived a life of freedom and adventure, so vastly different than her own routine, which she felt was not much better than the dreary existence of a prisoner, caged and bound.

When it became apparent that one of the truant girls had grown plump with child, the deflowered maiden was beaten so ferociously she lost the precious content of her fecund belly. It was on that pivotal day the young orphan named Llorenc pilfered what food and cutlery she could from the kitchens and departed the white walls of the Virgin, never to return.

Despite an intimate knowledge of the alleyways of Barcelona, the fact that Dolores could no longer find refuge within the monastery left her vulnerable to exposure in all its grueling forms. After barely escaping abduction and an attempt at rapine, she made her way to the boatyard, more specifically, L'aventure Joyeuse. The sleek caravel was not the most luxurious of ships that came and went from the docks, but it was kept relatively clean due to a diligent crew who radiated a most jolly disposition. Hiding away between the bulkheads, she made herself comfortable and scarce amidst the spare riggings. It was after a sleep deeper and more relaxing than she had been allowed for nearly a week, that she arose to find herself adrift upon the Tyrrhenian Sea, with Barcelona but a shining sliver fading along the horizon.

****

During a salt pork raid spurred on by a groaning stomach, Dolores's presence was abruptly discovered by one of the crewmates. Hoisted aloft and gut-punched by a brawny stevedore, the crafty stowaway was unceremoniously hauled above deck to await her punishment. The ship's men circled to the sounds of the commotion beneath the guiding stars that shone more brilliantly than any night the city could reveal.

In due time, a fur-robed and yawning figure emerged from the captain's quarters to perch in mock nonchalance before the dangling captive. His blond hair was cropped close to his scalp and a powder burn speckled the flesh beneath his right eye. Her captor deposited his catch upon the planked floor to be jeered and gawked at by the entirety of the crew. The extravagant leader smirked, seeming to take a perverse pleasure listening to the descriptive tortures his men spouted towards their squirming captive. He mulled over the variety of ex-traction procedures raucously shouted about, but his heart changed when he beheld her defiant and fearless stare. In a gracious, genteel manner, he lifted the shaken girl to her feet and introduced himself as Brim Jorge, former privateer of the French Monarchy and current head of *L'aventure Joyeuse*.

Taking her under his wing, or fur-lined cloak to be more accurate, Brim Jorge set the lithe girl to the crow's nest where she learned to scurry the ropes like a lemur, and the intricacies of knotwork necessary for any boat's man. The sailors swiftly grew fond of the bold orphan's refreshing naivete and youthful exuberance. They taught her games of chance, the ability to read the stars, and the vulgar, yet witty lingo that seamen are so well known for. Despite the stench of man sweat, soured sustenance, and crude habits of the ale-guzzling ruffians, Dolores found the freedom of the sea, paradoxically exhilarating and tranquil.

Her open and juvenile adaptability shaped instantaneous sea legs and buffered the abrupt change to her diet, environment, and company. The world changed, yet the malleable, inquisitive mind kept pace, through calm waters and tempestuous seas. The men were as diverse as the waters; the boisterous, rotund Sicilian cook, the swarthy, academic navigator from Morocco, a stern, mustachioed cannoneer of Hunnic descent, the flame-haired carpenter who everyone called the Nord. Yet it was the cloaked Frenchman that most intrigued her, with his panache and sense of novelty towards whatever may come his way.

The gregarious Jorge DuPonte doted upon his young ward as a father would, swathing her in foreign silks and linens… purple was her preferred hue. He made the attempt to train her wee arms in the use of the foil, but it was the pistol he kept tucked into his vermillion sash that best suited her innate proclivities. Brim Jorge allowed his sophomoric protégé to spend his musket shot discharging into the saltwater fishes as *L'aventure Joyeuse* traversed ever northward. The budding woman was a deadeye, a sure shot who managed to deliver a belly-up result nine out of ten times. But when the captain and his men partook too highly of the hops-water and began to fire heavy metal into the sleek bodies of the striped dolphins, with eyes so much like that of a fellow man, Dolores snuck her way to the Vieux-Port of Marseille when the ship docked. The first mate offered to haul the girl back aboard, but Jorge dismissed him, smiling ruefully towards the back of the fleeing Spaniard who captured his heart like none other.

****

Dolores Llorenc scurried through the bustling streets of Marseille in a bewildered frenzy of adrenaline, not knowing where here next steps would lead her. Without a coin she could call her own, the young lass was unable to satiate the emptiness of her stomach. So, she begged, and her sweet face, large eyes, and innocent demeanor worked for a span, but her pidgin French and Catalonian dialect would get her kicked and spat upon by those who held a deep-seated hatred towards the kingdom across the southern border. This led to her swiping from the edges of food vendors and fruit carts. Thievery sufficed for a handful of days until she made the unwise decision to return to a previous mark. The turnip-seller's son witnessed the sneak's fingers make purchase and gave chase down the alleys of France's most ancient city. His longer legs quickly overtook the teenage thief, and he unleashed such a beating that most of her face was left mottled and swollen.

The pain, shame, and trauma caused from the thrashing horrified Dolores enough to leave the city, deciding to take her chances on the rural countryside, an environment wholly unfamiliar to her limited range of experience. The initial outreaches of Marseille were tamed and sculpted enough to allow easy access to grapes and apples. Animal pens provided shelter and one generous family graciously fed her mutton and housed her for an evening, regaling her with tales of heredity and the countless generations that tended the acreage for centuries. That night she wept bitterly into wool sheets, for she never knew the caress of a mother or the embrace of a father. She had no heritage, knew no siblings, possessed absolutely nothing but the tattered threads that clung to her small frame. At dawn, she quietly departed the cozy domicile before any of its inhabitants arose to begin another day.

The landscape became more rugged, less manicured, as the weather grew harsh, bleak, and cold. Dolores swiped a horse blanket from a stable to subdue her shivering and teeth chattering. She moved ever eastward, using the sun's rise and the astronomy the Moroccan taught her to guide her steps. Civilization was now days away and when any cart or horseman came clopping down the trail, she dashed to the trees to hide in the woods. She knew well enough the dangers of being a lone woman in an unknown world.

The rains came and the thick cloth she wrapped herself in grew drenched and heavy with biting moisture. She scavenged what flower petals and blades of grass she could digest until she retched, purging herself painfully of all inedible material. Fear and despair kept her up all night despite debilitating weakness and severe exhaustion. She could feel her ribs through her shredded blanket as she stumbled across the forest in a hallucinatory state, unable to determine up from down. This addled mindset lasted for an unknown length of time until she collapsed in a pathetic heap beneath dead shrubbery.

****

Dolores awoke in a haze atop a luxurious four-post bed the likes of which she had never experienced before, but the severe belly cramps and throbbing in her temples forced her to take no comfort from the down bedding that bore her frail body. Concerned voices rattled through her traumatized brain as she was spoon fed broth.

Yellow fever

Syphilis

The plague

The time was lost to Dolores as she slipped in and out of consciousness. Fever dreams of abusive nuns, being hounded by gangs of hostile men, monsters in the sea and dragons in the woods haunted her delirium. The day finally came when she could raise her head from the fragrant pillows, a little at first, but enough strength returned to make her way to the toilet and intake solid food.

As she recovered, she learned she had been residing north of Cannes, in the resplendent villa of a Duchess with an unpronounceable name and was nursed back to health by the noblewoman's youngest daughter. Some weeks earlier, she had been discovered by the young woman's paramour and the stableboy, Pierre. The household took kindly to the tiny Catalonian, giggling at her lilting accent and rejoicing in her foreign mannerisms. The ladies-in-waiting pleated her luxuriant raven locks and garbed her in the current fashions of France's aristocracy.

It was during this time that Dolores was schooled in the courtly ways, perfecting her curtsey and grueling through the tedious process of hosting dinner parties for distinguished merchants and pampered nobles. Still, the exotic beauty could not help but feel stifled by the boring routines of shallow popinjays and stuffy traditionalists.

Whenever the opportunity arose, the girl from Barcelona sought the stables to find solace upon the sturdy backs of the Andalusians that swept her across the pastures in a union of speed and exhilaration. The marriage of rider and mount provided a rise and crest that transcended speciation into a oneness that could not be denied, as the whipping wind tore through her brunette braids. The sleek and beautiful colorations of the majestic creatures housed intricate and intelligent souls, and Dolores marveled at their individual personalities and the deepening bonds she forged with the herd.

Horsemanship also gave Dolores an opportunity to

spend time with Pierre, who shared an appreciation for her company as revealed by his blushes instigated by her toothsome smile. The young man had a humble and down-to-earth demeanor lacking amongst the intrigues and fineries of the hoity-toity. She found herself growing heated at his nearness and his touch stiffened the fine hairs of her forearms and nape of the neck. A day came when they ascended the barn's loft and atop a spilling of hay, she revealed herself for the first time to a male. She received him in awkward embraces… playful, fumbling, and thrilling. Their romantic tryst a shared secret kept hidden from the high-born, a clandestine meeting for the two alone.

Meanwhile, the Duchess's daughter, who was a wee bit older than Madame Llorenc, had begun to receive suitors for her hand in matrimony. The young woman of nobility had been caught by an untrustworthy confidante in the arms of her lover, and gossip began to circle of her illicit affair. The most jealous and hot-tempered of the competitors for the lady's hand caught wind of these rumors and appeared one climactic day with a horde of drunken supporters and bullies. He challenged the quaking paramour to a pistol duel and dishonorably unleashed a shot into the back of the ousted lover before he could finalize his tenth step.

Chaos ensued as the lover's corpse was desecrated with a beheading delivered by one of the inebriated infiltrators. This was followed by a savage takeover of the Duchess's estate with the intoxicated trespassers forcing their way inside, raiding the pantries and tormenting the women as the manservants were beaten or chased away.

When a fire was ignited within the villa, Pierre scooped up a stunned and horrified Dolores, riding hard with the inferno lighting their way into the night.

****

Dolores Llorenc entered the territory of Genoa a fully bloomed woman. Still petite in stature; her musculature, self-sufficiency, and confidence had reached an excelled potential she never would have envisioned during her sheltered childhood amongst the nuns. It was pleasant to smell the faint tinge of the sea breeze as she hopped off a merchant's wagon that graciously delivered her to the port-city as daylight neared its closure.

The young woman had fared well for herself along her escapades despite the obstacles and hardships that arose to hinder her path. Dolores and Pierre had ingratiated themselves with a pack of Roma nomads who allowed them to perform horse tricks for their travelling circus, Pierre taking the lead of the horse as his spry companion enacted handstands and cartwheels she learned from the tribe's acrobat. They parted ways with the caravan who steered their ornately painted carriages northward as the duo continued ever easterly, towards the uppermost edges of the gulf.

When their meagre finances dwindled, desperation took root, and Dolores concocted a scheme both brilliant and foolhardy. Portraying the part of damsel in distress as Pierre played the role of the nefarious assailant, the pair managed to catch the attention of a mercantile cart with their antics. Their plan to waylay the unsuspecting transport went horribly awry when the coachman grazed Pierre's midriff with the edge of his rapier. Adrenaline and animal instinct took control as Dolores shattered a fallen branch across the teamster's skull rendering him unconscious along the side of the roadway. With a strength born of primal despair, Dolores managed to drag her friend to the wagon and guide it to the nearest farmstead.

When Pierre regained consciousness, bandaged and weary upon a stranger's bed, he would not look his partner in the eye. He regretfully informed Dolores that he would not continue their journey and would remain in France, the only home he had ever known. She pleaded, sobbed, and promised the world, but alas, she could not sway her recalcitrant lover to budge his position. So, she gave her farewells and with a heavy heart, crossed the border towards the hub of Catholicism and birthland of the romantic languages.

Despite the loss of a boon companion, her first love and gentle friend, she entered this new realm, this new chapter of her story, with an openness and freedom that left no room for the fear and trepidation that had marked her juvenile years with such heightened uncertainty. So, she brushed the past aside, tipped the driver, and sauntered the Genoese streets with the sea to the south and the mountains framing her view to the north. As the sun set behind her, she made her way into the heart of the city by streetlight and the crescent moon smiling down from above.

****

JASIAH WITKOFSKY

After grounding herself with a hearty beef stew from a quaint little establishment, Dolores resumed her stroll through the city by night, too enamored with the bustling seaside array to think of bedding down. Her studies in Latin made the Italian dialect less of a challenge than the flow of the French, and she ascertained that she could easily call a place such as this her home. An abode both comfortable, yet exciting, with its constant sea traffic importing an endless array of exotic goods and people from around the globe.

Meandering through the cobbles and wagon ruts, Dolores became aware of a raucous commotion from above. On a rooftop balcony four-stories high, she made out a small revelry alit with lanterns and braziers. There was no stairway or ladder to access the merriment, just a drainpipe bolted to the wall, so, strapping her satchel securely over her shoulder, she began the ascent. As she reached the top and hopped the rail, she saw a dozen rascals, ruffians, and rapscallions of various sorts. Their only commonality was the bright red scarves wrapped around heads, waists, or limbs.

The party did not detect her presence at first, but as she boldly approached, they sprang to their feet brandishing wide-bladed daggers in her direction. When they realized the intruder was nothing more than a petite, unarmed woman, the man nearest to her motioned the gang to lower their weaponry. The flickering lights shone against the man's deeply bronzed flesh and stringy chin beard as he eyed the newcomer up and down. His attire was a hodge-podge of faded rags and flamboyant sashes that secured an ornate saber to his side, but the surrounding members of the gathering seemed to hold this eccentric character in some regard, so they allowed him to speak for them.

"How did you get up here, *ragazza*?"

With open-mouthed, wide-eyed honesty, Dolores responded. "I climbed."

The conglomeration of rogues nodded and chuckled, impressed by the fearless audacity of the uninvited guest. Taking the queue, the man continued, "And can we have the Madame's name?"

"Dolores Llorenc." she stammered, "I am new here. I just arrived from the west today."

The man responded with a flourishing bow, "Madame Llorenc, I am Signore Jerome, and we are the Crimson Cinquedeas. Cavaliers unranked and currently dismounted. Men of novel virtue and particular skills." This final remark brought hearty guffaws from the scoundrels behind him. Grabbing a bottle from a stool, the swarthy man handed it to her. "If you are to grace us with your beautiful presence, then you must drink with us."

Not wanting to be rude, she took a swig and immediately coughed out the sour and rancid-tasting liquid, the worst wine she had ever tasted. The party exploded in laughter at her response, but not wishing to be humiliated, she took a three-gulp swill and managed to swallow it down before handing it back, swiping drops from her chin and giving Jerome a steely glance. He offered the young woman his seat and a bowl of pistachios as the men introduced themselves and questioned her lightly about her history.

Jerome, who the scoundrels teasingly labeled 'the Moor' for his deep skin tone, narrow eyes, and beaked nose, took interest in the orphan's curious tale and when he learned of her brief nautical stint, his wine-addled mind brewed a scheme to recruit her into their numbers.

"*Ragazza*, we like your spirit. It would be an honor if you were to join our company. Would you like to wear the crimson?"

Taken aback by the request, she blurted out a response before thinking, "Ye…Yes…" not realizing the predicament she stepped into.

He raised a brow flirtatiously, "We are a loyal and leaderless organization, but to bear the red requires proof of your mettle and acumen. Would you take it upon yourself to perform a quest for us?"

Not wishing to disappoint the first people she met in this coastal city, and possibly emboldened by the strong vintage, she attempted a response to match the wits of this overdressed freebooter. "It depends on what said mission requires. I do have standards and as a follower of Christ, I will not harm another."

Stroking his dark chin scruff, Jerome turned towards the docks, easily visible from their rooftop vantage and pointed to a particular merchant's vessel. "You see that ship yonder, fair Madame? Being a man of fine tastes and high aesthetics, I would consider it a noteworthy gift if you were to return to us with that purple flag upon the mast. Since you snuck upon us so silently and have worked the nest previously, such an endeavor should be no problem for one of your talents. Am I correct in this estimation?"

She internally debated the proposition, the risks versus rewards, then nodded her agreement to Jerome's weather-beaten face.

"One more thing, Madame." He handed her a broad-bladed dagger, the namesake of their gang. "Do not get caught…and do not name us."

****

In a narrow crevice between two building, Dolores removed her skirts and donned her dark stockings and black corset, stuffing her bag in a large crack in the plaster. She tied her hair tightly behind her, then made her way through the winding streets. She reached the docks and surveyed both sides of the ship, *L'orgoglio del Seno*. She made out one guard upon the vessel resting amidst an amalgamation of sacks, his cap was low on his face, but she could make out a pistol strapped to his rotund midriff.

The midnight hour was approaching, and the waxing moon was now low in the sky. She took advantage of the low visibility to crawl hand over hand on the connecting rope that secured the vessel to the dock. As silently as she could be, she slipped over the rail and scurried to the shadows of the stern.

The guard did not move at all, so Dolores assumed he was asleep. She made sure the wide blade was attached firmly to the lacings of her corset, then climbed the rigging at the back of the ship. She was calm and sure in her movements, keeping the bundled sails between her and the sleeping man, obfuscating her presence as much as possible. She attained the mizzenmast but did not think she had the strength to scurry the line between her current position and the mainmast which bore the lightly billowing flag the bandit gang desired.

Dolores mustered all her courage and began to slowly saw the rope with the dagger gifted to her. When a few threads were the only thing holding the rope in place, she drew in a deep breath and lunged, gripping the twined cordage for dear life as her weight severed the rope and sent her swinging straight towards the largest beam of the ship. She used her feet to cushion the impact of collision into the wooden pillar, and froze in position, terrified and breathless.

Her straining palms and fading strength signaled she had limited time to pull off this caper. Risking a glance, she blew a sigh of relief to find that she had not been observed yet, so with frog-like bounds, she scaled the mast to the top. With a few savage hacks, she managed to free the purple flag, which began to flutter away from her. In desperation, she dropped the blade to clutch the flag which almost escaped her swift grasp.

The clatter of the steel cinquedea upon the deck woke the guard as Dolores slid down the mainmast to hide amidst the gathered sails. As the man waddled beneath her to pick up the object that roused him from his slumber, she dropped, using the folds of the sailcloth to soften her descent. When the dark-clad female thudded amidship by his side, the surprised ship's guard was so startled he dropped the dagger. She took advantage of his momentary paralysis to pull the pistol from the man's shoulder strap, cock the device, and aim it straight at his heart.

"Not one word." She exhaled, both infiltrator and guard wide-eyed with fear. Never had she been in the position of a standoff, gun in one hand, flag in the other. She took careful steps backwards till she made the ship's edge, then scurried down the plank to the dock below, running as fast as her feet allowed.

The man's cries for help turned the few heads that were about at this late hour. The frightened thief wrapped the flag around the firearm, then plunged into the sea. She awkwardly paddled one-armed towards the shore and clutched the rocky edge, catching her breath beneath the dock as shipmen and patrols scurried about looking for the burglar. Since swimming was not a skill that she had developed well, she hugged the shoreline and quietly drifted away from the scene of the crime.

When the Barcelonan thought she had an opportunity, she scurried to dry ground and bolted towards the city. She knew she had been spotted as screams followed her through the streets. Exhausted and unable to catch her breath, she searched desperately for dark and unoccupied regions of this foreign land she knew nothing about. She thanked the Angels and the Virgin when she discovered a covered wagon – the perfect place to hide. She dove inside, stilled her breathing, and prayed that no one heard her thundering heart as the hurried steps of several pursuers ran past her place of concealment.

She recited twenty Hail Marys and the Lord's Prayer thrice before braving a glimpse outside the cart. With the street empty, she slid out and tried to retrace her steps as best she could in this strange, urban maze. She stayed in the shadows whenever possible and avoided human contact, knowing that a lone, half-dressed female, nervously walking the night would be a suspicious and scandalous affair.

Tired, scared, and frustrated, Dolores found herself lost and backtracking for what must have been hours before luck or divine providence brought her back to the tight alley that concealed her satchel and clothing. She dressed herself and tucked the waterlogged pistol into her tote bag before pacing back to the rooftop hideout of the Crimson Cinquedeas.

She nearly screamed her heart out when she was muffled and pulled into an alley by a burlap-laden assailant. The man, who was garbed as a leper, hissed for her to remain silent before releasing her as he instructed Dolores to don the rags he shoved into her arms. He then led her into a broad thoroughfare, motioning for her to follow closely. Terrified, but with nowhere else to turn, she had no choice but to trust this stranger. Tears began to stream down her cheeks as she sought some option, some means of escape, for she had no idea where her abductor was taking her.

When marching steps were heard coming towards their direction, the man pulled her roughly to a sitting position against a brick wall. He pulled a bowl from his rags and held it out like a beggar would as a patrol of armed guardsmen stomped into view. The constabulary steered clear from the two, one spitting in disgust at their general direction. When the guards passed by, her mysterious savior pulled her to her feet and continued leading her to some unknown destination.

THE PURPLE PISTOLLERA

****

"You thought we would abandon you, *ragazza*?"

Jerome's exuberant voice startled Dolores as he called down to her from a window above. "You sure ran Raphael there on a wild chase." The man who had brought her here withdrew a key from his shredded attire and opened a door before her. Ushering Dolores inside, she found herself within what appeared to be an unoccupied warehouse. The man called Raphael, who she now recognized as one of the rooftop revelers, led her up a stairwell to a gutted room where Jerome sat on an array of rugs with other Cinquedeas, smoking New World tobacco from a pipe.

"Do you bear gifts for us, Madame Llorenc?" Jerome smirked, offering a small pillow for her to sit upon.

Rifling through her satchel, she dropped the purple cloth and captured pistol upon the pile of strewn carpets. Whistling in amazement, Jerome examined the firearm, before passing it on to a companion. "Well done, very well done Madame. Regale us with your escapade, for we love nothing more than a good retelling of an adventure."

She told of her endeavors, too breathless to add flourishes and embellishments. The Cinquedeas eyed her with a newfound respect as they popped open another jug of deep red wine. The drunken rogues related some of their own tales of initiation as they fed her skewered chicken and vegetables.

Jerome withdrew a crimson bandana and with exaggerated fluttering, offered it to the Spaniard. "You exceeded all expectations, and you are now one of us, Madame Llorenc."

She swiped the cloth and retorted, "And how do I know that you would do for me what I just risked for you? I placed my very existence in jeopardy to please your whims. How do I know that you would do likewise?"

Jerome rose, placing his hand over his heart, feigning wounded pride. "Why upon my honor, my dear. I am ever at your service…Madame Pistollera. I think that is what I will call you. If you need anything, and it is within my power to give…then it shall be yours. You have my word, and you have my sword." He drew his saber with a flourish, slashing at the air before him.

The others joined in their praises and promises, each trying to outdo their fellows in pomp and gallantry. She found herself growing fond of their jovial, immature antics. Jerome hung the captured flag outside the window as the bottle was passed about until its contents were completely emptied. When Dolores gave a deep yawn, Jerome ushered his inebriated compatriots towards the door. "You can have this room, for this night is yours, my pretty Pistollera…unless you wish me to stay and keep you company?" He raised an eyebrow in anticipation.

"Is that a proposal? Do you have a ring for me, Jerome?" she countered.

He chuckled as he reached the doorway. "There will be more nights, more opportunities, more chances for you to change your mind. But tomorrow, the day is yours. We shall await your presence, Madame." With a sweeping bow he closed the door behind him.

As she blew out the assortment of candles that lit the room, she tucked the crimson cloth beneath her weary head as she lay herself down upon the pile of rugs. The last thing she saw before shutting her eyes was the purple merchant's flag fluttering outside the window. It was nice to be a part of something larger than herself, but there would soon come a day when she would fly her own colors. The faint aftertaste of the wine upon her lips was bittersweet…a fitting metaphor for existence. Life held pain, its deep tragedies and heart-rending losses, but it was also a wondrous adventure, to savor and enjoy.

THE RED RICASSO
&
ORIGINS OF THE CRIMSON CINQUEDEAS

Upon the rooftop of *La Tettarella del Drago*, Genoa's premiere hostel, tavern, and brothel, a private revelry was being held under the moon and Mediterranean stars. A select crowd of red-scarved individuals, their lovers, and a petite woman strapped within an amethyst corset and topped beneath a gigantic cavalier's hat, enjoyed relaying puffed-up deeds of heroism and bravado in a state of growing intoxication. Flagons and carafes passed amongst the gathering, washing down the breads and sweet meats with wine and ale as men of skill juggled, jigged, and displayed acrobatic feats escalating in risk and flamboyance.

After one braggadocio's hilarious string of comedic slurs came to an end and the raucous laughter died down, the little woman with the large hat chimed in. "Jerome, since you are one of the eldest in attendance…"

"Yet young at heart, *ragazza*." The ugly, bearded man interrupted his friend, Dolores, amidst the dwindling chuckles of the partygoers.

"I was curious, Jerome." She continued, "If anyone here were to know, I figured it would be you. How did your band of Crimson Cinquedeas come into formation? There is no established leadership, no organization save this structure where we all conglomerate. It seems so organic, like birthed from nature as a species, as if your group has been here since the dawn of time."

"Well, Madame Pistollera. This is quite the story, so everyone gather round and perk your ears in my direction." The surly Tuscan quaffed a hefty stream of ale before taking a deep breath to address his audience.

"There are myths of Etruscan origins, an ancient warrior cult that soaked their headcloths in the blood of horses for the sake of their Gods and Goddesses, long lost to time. Some claim there was a rebellious counterculture that went underground during Constantine's Christian proclamation…a splinter Mithras sect that defied the Roman conversion to Catholicism.

"But the only definitive history we can derive comes some two hundred years ago – that might not seem like a long time, but the world was a far more primitive and darker place back then. Before Colombo's discovery of America, the Medici art revolution, and Magellan's circumnavigation of the globe. Swords were longer and significantly broader, like the blade used by the protagonist of our little fable – the Red Ricasso!"

Jerome drew his saber with a flourish, a fitting prop for his 'historical' retelling. "The Red Ricasso was said to be an exiled noble, or a liege-less knight, or a lone survivor from a mercenary contingent, exact origins matter little for his birthname has become lost to the ages. What is pertinent are the heroic deeds of his formidable years.

"You may ask, how did this mysterious figure receive his *nom de guerre*? It was during one of his greatest battles when he was ambushed by a half dozen aggressors. He managed to kill or wound five of the bullies, but one of his jumpers came in too close, forcing the Ricasso to take the man's eye with the thin, foremost spoke of his hilt. Those who did not flee bled out in the streets and the Ricasso's blade was coated blood-red from tip to grip…like I said, a more brutal era."

All the while, Jerome pantomimed the actions of the gang's patron-saint with his broad-bladed saber as he continued his reenactment. "At some point, the Ricasso acquired an underling…a sidekick if you prefer. He was a short and wily fellow called Piero the Knife, and he helped keep their bellies full with his burglary and gambling. Now, the Ricasso did not treat Piero all that well, whether it be the knifeman's lower station, shorter size, coarser features…whatever the reasons, that would all come to change.

"During one of their many capers, the two virtuous villains found themselves surrounded by one gang amongst their numerous rivals. Typical of their exceptional skills and cunning, the Ricasso and the Knife dispatched or made cowards of their foes. Yet, one such craven hid in a nearby alley and when the duo passed by, he lunged forth to backstab the Red Ricasso. The blow would have been fatal, but it never made contact, for Piero's sharp ears caught the man's steps, and he managed to thrust his trusty cinquedea deep into the assailant's gut."

That being told, Jerome produced the five-fingers width knife with his offhand. "From that day forward, the Ricasso would treat his friend and savior with full respect, as an equal unparalleled. Hence the reason we have no leaders, for all men are their own and worthy in one manner or another.

"They would go on to gather more cohorts, imitators, and savory scoundrels of variety and particular talents. No man lives forever, so others would go on to don his mask and red cape, further continuing his legend, but none other would have the bevy of escapades and daunting experiences as the original warrior-rogue.

So, we find ourselves here today. In honor of the Red Ricasso and Piero the Knife, we wear the crimson and carry the cinquedea…hallmarks of our trade as inheritors of the noble lineage of what are arguably the greatest rapscallions of this realm's glorious history. We terrorize the rich and spit upon the royals, keeping our eyes peeled for noteworthy individuals to carry on our righteous racket of rascality into further generations yet to come, forming an alternative family for the disenfranchised misfits of might and merit.

"And with that…my story comes to a finale." Crossing his arms, Jerome drove his blades into their scabbards with simultaneous slicing sounds. He followed his performance with a low bow to his audience of ruffians and flirtatious femme fatales who applauded his orations and extravagant gesticulations. The storyteller tore a jug from one of his mate's hands to wet his weary tongue.

Dolores, sitting upon a crate stack, fingered her chin thoughtfully. "Despite your penchant for hyperbole, exaggeration, and tall-tales…I am willing to give your story some credence. You gave multiple options rather than overconfidently claiming absolute knowledge of events that have transpired which you have not personally witnessed and have been passed down as folklore. So, thank you for answering my inquiry with such gusto and honest uncertainty."

Shaking beer foam from his stringy beard, Jerome eyed Dolores with narrowed lids. "Thank you…I think…?"

The feasting, drinking, pipe-smoking, jesting, and dancing commenced into the later hours. Mock duels and inebriated philosophical debates ensued while most of the port-city slept and dreamt, secure in their domiciles. The rooftop shenanigans continued until a shout from below shattered the frivolity several stories high.

"Come down! All of you! No fires on the roofs past midnight!"

From above, onlookers gazed down to observe those who interrupted the skyline merrymaking. On the streets below stood a patrol of authorities prepared to detain the revelers on high. One of the painted ladies turned to her friends to warn of the situation at ground level.

"It is Conestabile Aldo and his gaggle of brutes, intent on disrupting our menagerie."

Cleto, the brawniest – and drunkest – approached the ledge to hurl an emptied ceramic wine vessel at the platoon seeking to break up the party. His aim was off, and the earthenware jug exploded in a clatter on the cobbles at the feet of the Conestabile, but the offense was enough to enrage the squadron.

"You are now in violation of threatening and assaulting officers of peace within the good city of Genoa! Descend the lot of you and we will not be forced to apprehend your worthless, miserable carcasses!" The leader of the law enforcers screeched at the top of his lungs.

The rooftop curfew-breakers jeered down at the upholders of legality, taunting and dousing the city's guardians with the remaining vestiges of the vintages they imbibed. At their wick's end, the constabulary produced a long wooden ladder to scale up to the group of rambunctious transgressors of propriety.

While this back-and-forth interaction occurred, Dolores had enough time to load her pistol with powder and lead. Taking careful aim, she discharged her firearm into the middle of one of the ladder's legs, rendering the climbing implement useless. Stowing the smoking gun into her lavender sash, she cried out to her crew of conspicuous conspirators.

"Hurry! Gather your belongings and flee! No time to dillydally or match wits with step-in-line officials! We must escape!"

The partakers of perennial pranks and pernicious petulance took to their heels, making their escape jumping roofs, crossing planks, and swing down cordage to avenues or windows of obscurity. Hoots of laughter and celebratory exaltation echoed off the stone and plaster walls of the streets of Genoa as the Crimson Cinquedeas and the Purple Pistollera scattered into the night.

BLOODED BLADES & BLEEDING HEARTS
THE STRUCTURES OF ENGAGEMENT

PROLOGUE

The War of the Mantuan Succession was a significant portion of the greater Thirty Years War, a drawn-out conflict as the name suggests, that dragged the entirety of Europe into the battlefield, whether directly or otherwise. A devastating and divisive outcome of the Reformation period where millions died as a result of the newly formed Protestant movement gaining traction in the north, encroaching further into lands that were previously under the Catholic religious monopoly that held sway for a millennium.

When the last male heir to the Mantua duchy passed away, a proxy war erupted between the nations of the Spanish Habsburgs of the fractured Holy Roman Empire, fighting for their routes of transport through the northern Italian states, contested by the French Bourbons. This latter division sponsored Charles Gonzaga, Duke of Nevers and cousin to the deceased Duke, as the Spaniards backed Ferrante II Gonzaga, another distant cousin and Duke of Guastalla, both essentially puppet-lords with ambitions of their own.

The various Italian providences chose their sides individually and Genoa decided to pull its forces behind Spain, being the closest of the city-states to the southern Habsburg kingdom. Ambrogio Spinola, the First Marquess of Los Balbases and Genoese nobleman of the Republic, was granted Captain-Generalship by the Spanish to replace Gonzalo Fernandez de Cordoba in the siege of the pivotal city of Casale Monferrato. Along the way, there was a massive recruitment of soldiers throughout the Republics of Italy.

But enough of this history lecture…let the story commence…

CAST OF CHARACTERS

Dolores Llorenc sat on the balcony of *La Tettarella del Drago* with her new lover, Lucius Bernaldo DiCappa, viewing the moonlit city in each other's embraces. It was warm for an early spring night in Genoa, the city that kissed the coast, so they wore little and kept each other close. Dolores spun the residual swill at the bottom of the carafe signaling the need for a refill. Lucius sighed as he threw on a loose overshirt and proceeded downstairs to refill the pitcher.

Dolores leaned against the latticed rail, letting the breeze gently graze her dark, full hair and reflected upon how good life had treated her in this fair city. She was surprised how much she enjoyed a relaxing, pleasant existence. Years spent in constant agitation, always on the tips of her toes, never knowing where her next steps would lead her… she had become so accustomed to the chaotic path of the adventurer, she never imagined that settled relaxation would be anything save drool and boring. Yet, for once, she found contentment as enjoyable as excitement. What had come over her, she chuckled?

Her paramour; young, handsome, poised and gallant…could she possibly bed down in a homestead with this fair one and bear children? This man with the heart-melting smile and touch so soothing…she found herself at peace for the very first time.

As the chill of the evening set in, she clutched her

shawl over her shoulders and wondered why her lover was taking so long.

Meanwhile, Lucius flirted with the waitstaff as he had the vessel topped with fresh wine. He slapped the posteriors of the barmaids as they passed and continued to regale the busty keep with exaggerations of his family's exploits, seeming to forget the half-dressed woman above whom he courted.

Jerome the Moor, wrapped up his losing streak at card games, scowling down at his meagre stack of coins, then up at the despicable lot that frequented his favored establishment. He was in a surly mood this evening as he shifted to a personal table, pulling out a sheet of scrawled paper to further finesse his prose. After adding some ale to his inkwell to make the precious liquid carry further, he carved the flaky residue from the tip of his quill with one of several blades he kept constantly at his side.

When words failed him, he would glare at the belligerent crowd; the sloppy drunks, lusting grifters, and scrawny young nobles poorly attempting to prove their machismo to each other. He tried to draw inspiration for his dark, tragic musings, when Dolores descended from her chambers to drape herself over her new lover, Jerome didn't care to remember his name. Her quick eyes noticed her friend brooding in the corner, so she whispered in her paramour's ear and approached her comrade.

"Why the long look, Jerome, did you try your poor luck at cards again? Need coin for ale?" She teased her sour companion.

"Bah, *ragazza.* I have enough to get plenty drunk if

need be. But I am glad to see your beautiful face. Maybe if you are around more to watch over me, I would not be in such miserable straits." He taunted the woman in return.

"I have been spending all of my time with Lucius before he sets out to join the ranks of the military. The situation in the north has grown quite dire as of late, and he bravely follows the path of his fathers to fight the noble cause." She swooned, "He will make all of Genoa proud, and he says that when he returns, he will ask my hand for matrimony."

Her scarred and swarthy friend scoffed through his beard, "Huh, my father may own an estate, but that doesn't mean I do. I don't trust this man you have fallen so carelessly for. He is too pretty to be a warrior. No scars…no calluses…"

Dolores interrupted Jerome's badmouthing rant, "You don't have to be so obvious in your jealousies, Jerome. How dare you make such presumptions about the man I love? Is this how you treat friends just because you are having a bad go at it?"

"Just a warning, *ragazza*." Jerome shrugged, "I trust my eyes, they have served me well, and I will never lie to you about what I see."

"And I will always tell you my truth, Jerome. And at this moment you are being petty and envious. This is why you spend your time alone in a corner, scribbling hate and gloom on dirty napkins. I hope you get good rest tonight and wake up the jovial friend whom I adore so dearly. Until then, stay away from making actions out of your opinions and interfere not with my engagements."

Jerome watched his partner-in-crime depart back to her quarters, amore in tow. His mood did not grow any lighter after the encounter as he mused over his jottings. "May my predictions be proven wrong, *ragazza*. I say what I say out of care, and if your heart breaks, then we all lose." He mumbled to himself as his mug was refilled and the night deepened.

INTRO

fervent crowd gathered under the bright midday sun to send off the armed men enlisted to fight for Mantua and Montferrat possession. Emotions ran strong yet varied amidst the audience witnessing the departure of young recruits and weathered veterans. Patriotic cheers for the brave and honorable mixed with the wails of the mothers who had previously lost a child to combat, fearing that another would become fodder for the blood-fueled engines of war.

The pomp and formations of the marching soldiers, garbed in pristine uniforms and stepping in time to the battery of drums, stirred the fanfare of the city. The marchers were preceded by the ranks of the generals and cavaliers on horseback, banners marking divisions, heraldry, and flags of Genoa and allied nations, fluttered in the coastal breeze.

Upon one such noble steed rode Lucius Bernaldo DiCappa. Though he had never been blooded by involvement in battle, his family lineage granted him rank that was a privilege most soldiers would have to earn. He waved and flashed his winning smile to the onlookers, granting a special salute to a particular lady with a rooftop vantage.

Dolores Llorenc stood on high, waving her enormous musketeer's hat and blowing kisses to the man who rode off for an indefinite number of months.

years? As he cantered past, she stared at the back of her potential fiancé with a rising trepidation for the man of her dreams. She had spent the last few days blissed out, too enraptured in the budding general's words of romance and tender embraces to truly comprehend the ramifications of siege warfare. Now, these thoughts and feelings flooded in the gaps formerly filled with affection and wild abandonment to pleasure.

Kissing the cross worn about her neck, she wiped the tears from her eyes and left the rooftop for her private dwelling below. There were reservations and responsibilities she had to attend on her own before she could once again reunite with her love. She prepared herself for her duties and the distance that would separate her from the fair-haired man she esteemed so highly.

SETTING

The soldiers trekked towards the well-trodden Spanish Road, northwards to the base of the great Alps, making a good clip despite the cannons and supply trains that had to be dragged across rivers and uneven terrain. The city of Casale Monferrato along the Po River was heavily fortified and prepared for a continuation of the previous siege.

Lucius Bernaldo DiCappa was given a small contingent of recruits and sappers to perform the lowly and grueling task of mucking out and expanding one of the trenches that surrounded the besieged city. DiCappa whipped his men to a fervid pace in their duties, wishing to be done with demeaning chores so he could enter the battle proper. He envisioned glorified fantasies upon horseback, cavalier's saber in hand, leading a charge as he slashed enemy combatants out of his path and scattering fleeing townsfolk from his noble trajectory.

Meanwhile, back at the Genovese home front, Dolores had departed to the neighboring ports of Santa Margherita Ligure to use her wiles in service of her benefactors. With the loss of so many of the able-bodied menfolk of Genoa, the Sappone brothers saw this as an ample opportunity to enlarge their turf amidst the seedy underbelly of the city's winding alleys. They gathered their lackeys and bullied vendors and shopkeepers to pay a certain "homage" for forced acknowledgments of their imposed sovereignty.

Jerome glowered over his tankard at the growing presence of the Sappone gang who became so cocksure that they now felt confident enough to infiltrate *La Tettarella del Drago* in bulk. The elder, Bruno, became the loudest voice inside the tavern, paying for his men's inebriation and boasted thinly veiled proclamations of primary patronage for the inn and the surrounding districts. The younger Antonio poured ale over the half-covered breasts of the waitresses, trying to lap the frothing liquid like a thirst-stricken dog, and breaking mugs whenever rejected in his advances.

The help of the establishment grudgingly accepted the belligerent behavior of the Sappones, calculating that the cost paid out by the scoundrels was greater than the losses suffered by their reckless antics. Nevertheless, Jerome warned his band of Crimson Cinquedeas of the rising threat of the encroaching presence of the rival gang. He implored his merry fellows to keep eyes vigilant, and hands ready for steel.

CONFLICT

The time for preparations had come to a surprising and abrupt end with the sudden thunder of cannon-shot and the cracking reports of musketry. Lucius Bernaldo DiCappa was roused from a pleasant nap by the unexpected explosions that forced him to spring to his feet with a startled cry.

Lucius received a briefing of the situation from a recruit as he hastily buttoned his uniform and fitted his sword to his side. He was informed that messengers were sent from Spinola and the generals on high to all the minor officers in charge, and DiCappa was nowhere to be found. Lucius cursed his luck rather than his own breach of duty for the circumstances he now found himself in the middle of. Praying this infraction would be overlooked, he ordered his informant to lead him back to his deployment.

Although he had pushed his men hard in their workloads, he now regretted the state of the barricades he was assigned. No longer could he trot his horse into the rough cut of the unfinished trenches and the half-formed artificial banks were still not high enough to protect any man, unless they cowered supine and ineffective.

Lucius suddenly wished he could turn back the arc of time, paying more attention to his military instructors his parents hired for his tutelage. He excelled at his riding lessons, fared well with a blade, and managed to dis guise discipline with poise and presentation. But these skills were all individualistic, he never understood the necessity of transforming his natural charisma into true leadership. His grasp of tactics and strategy was paltry at best, and at this very moment, had entirely escaped his memory.

Lucius snapped back into reality by a cannonball that exploded all too near, raining down shredded sod upon him and his whinnying steed. Brushing off the detritus from the stark whites of his attire, Lucius demanded his go-between to bring back intelligence from the higher-ups, to know when and where to advance his charge. As the messenger sped off, Lucius reared his horse back out of harm's way, staring off at Casale, paralyzed by grave indecision.

That evening in Genoa, Jerome meandered the streets with a handful of his fellow Crimson Cinquedeas, intoxicated and making their way between various establishments, playing games of chance and imbibing the variety of foods and brews…as was their way.

Jerome puffed upon his pipe of stale tobacco from the New World as he told ribald jokes to his comrades in the blunt and swaggering manner that was his trademark, never failing to send those of a raucous nature to fall on their seats in tear-jerking laughter. Dragging each other about the streets and guffawing uproariously along the way back to their territory.

Noticing the uncharacteristically emptied street they turned into, Jerome had just enough time to stow his smoking apparatus away, signaling a warning to his companions, and gripping the broad-bladed dagger that was a hallmark of their band of rogues and rapscallions. A small horde of men entered the roadways before and behind them, cutting off any routes of departure for their ensnared prey. Jerome turned to Siero to hiss out to the youngest and swiftest of their small party.

"Lad! On my mark, run like the hare! Get your hide to the rest of us and tell them they are needed."

The Crimson Cinquedeas proceeded onward as if there was no impediment until addressed by Bruno, senior member of the Sappones.

"Your red doilies make you easy marks, ladies." The bruiser cracked his knuckles ominously, "You all are too dense to notice the shift in the winds. No longer do the western streets belong to the Cinquedeas. In fact, the entirety of Genoa no longer wishes your presence in town. After tonight, you will understand what you were too stupid to heed before. Men…" Bruno snapped his fingers.

"Siero! Now!" Jerome spun in place and launched a dart-sized knife into the arm of one of the men behind him. Siero followed the path of the thrown blade, weaving between his aggressors with all the agility of a wildcat, and bolted into the night.

Jerome turned to feel the biting steel of Bruno's rapier tear across his cheek and temple. He cursed his own negligence for leaving his trusty saber behind and took a defensive stance against his opponent.

Knowing his fellows were outnumbered as he heard the ring of steel and tussle of blows about him, Jerome fought like a cornered tiger…all he must do was stay on his feet till reinforcements arrived. His wide-bladed cinquedea parried the thrust of the rapier numerous times, but Bruno was a larger man with a longer blade, and his greater reach was beginning to wear Jerome down. A glancing blow to his hip drove Jerome to one knee, who was then forced on all fours by a hilt-punch to the side of his left eye.

Jerome was kicked several times in the gut before assistance rushed in to save their overwhelmed comrades. They pursued the ambushers who turned tail and fled, howling jeers and taunts as they ran, satisfied with the damage laid down upon the Crimson Cinquedeas. Jerome hacked wheezing coughs, unleashed the contents of his stomach, and fell upon the cobbles to stare helplessly at the bloody corpse of his friend and compatriot, Enzo. The stubborn and ferocious Jerome reached for his felled associate with a trembling hand before closing his eyes and losing consciousness.

CLIMAX

Jerome spent the next day and a half recovering from his cuts and bruises, and during the end of the second night, he gathered those who wore the crimson to *La Tettarella del Drago* to determine the best strategy forward. Be it pride, or simple necessity, or vengeance for the life of Enzo and those injured, the gathering of outlaws unanimously agreed to defend their long-held territory, like native born wolves keeping stray dogs at bay. It was instinctual…primal, where place and person had become one.

They pinned their demands to the door of the Sappone complex with the blade of the deceased Enzo…a clear symbol of honor and revenge. If the challenge was not accepted, then the Sappone name would be forever marred by cowardice and a lack of valor, unfit to frequent the domains of the underworld, for even the lawless retained a code.

The call was answered, and when the predetermined evening arrived, the Sappone gang made proper preparations, no firearms, just sharpened blades and fisticuffs, the way of the streets.

The Sappone gang made their way to neutral grounds, but at every turn, they found tassels of deep red tied to every flagpole, laundry line, and protrusion lining their way. The display of pomp and territory unnerved some of the town's bullies, but Bruno and Antonio Sappone kept their men in check, browbeating their followers to keep in tow and show no fear.

They met their rivals in an empty alley positioned in a rarely traversed side of town. The Crimson Cinquedeas, an ad hoc, brightly sashed band of anarchists and rascals, squared off with the Sappone brothers, their cousins, and tagalongs in a battle to determine primacy of the district…the loser would pack up and leave town, as arranged by the compact of the duel.

Jerome, one eye swollen and still limping from injuries dealt out earlier in the week, was prepared this night with his drawn saber, a broad blade, wider than the current style of curved swords worn by the cavalry. A weapon forged in a more Eastern style, reminiscent of the blades utilized by the Turks or the scimitars carried by the Arabians.

Giuseppe, being the most well-spoken of the Cinquedeas, addressed the Sappone gang when they came within earshot. "Less than a week ago, you brutally ambushed a small contingent of our brethren, leaving one of us dead on the streets. This is just a single example of numerous cases of extortion, bullying, and terrorization you have meted out upon our fair city. Your petty attempts at tyranny end now,"

The Cinquedeas proclamation was punctuated with the ringing of dozens of blades being drawn from scabbards. The Sappones likewise readied their weapons and both sides charged, screeching their battle cries. Whether to keep the constabulary away, or lack of affordability, no firearms were brandished, and the turf war was engaged as a hand-to-hand melee.

Jerome singled out the man who beat him unfairly before, and clashed steel with Bruno once again…this time, he was armed with more than just a simple dagger. Bruno was a significantly larger man, but that never halted Jerome's steps in the past. Since Bruno fought with a rapier, his style utilized a variety of piercing thrusts, techniques superior in the crowded alleyways. But Jerome was a scarred veteran, and knew how to keep his slashes quick and short.

Taking advantage of the long, bright red sash around his waist, Jerome dodged a low jab to his midriff and with his offhand, twined the cloth around Bruno's blade, taking control of the weapon. He delivered a paralyzing slice to his opponent's exposed bicep, then continued to bludgeon Bruno's bulbous nose over and over with the handguard of his saber. The vessels in contact burst all over Bruno's face, blinding him with his own blood and driving him to the ground.

Jerome sash-whipped the rapier out of Bruno's hand and straddled the prone figure, glaring down at the leader of the Sappones. "You should have finished me when you had the chance. Now, you shall never bully those you consider lesser again." Jerome took the pommel of his sword and shattered the connective knuckles of every digit of Bruno's dominant hand, tears streaking the blood and snot that smeared his face.

The gang war came to a closure as Bruno's younger sibling, Antonio, was dragged to the fore while the remaining members of the Sappones fled. Jerome gripped Bruno's curls and pulled his face up to stare directly at his terrified brother. "A life for a life, Bruno. And let this be done."

The man who held the captive drew his dagger and sliced Antonio's throat as his elder brother screamed in anguish and futility. The Crimson Cinquedeas raised their weapons on high and cheered their victory, the streets of Genoa were undisputed once more. They made way to celebrate at *La Tettarella del Drago*, leaving Bruno weeping over his brother's lifeless body.

Far to the north, the siege of attrition lingered on at the banks of Casale Monferrato. Lucius Bernaldo DiCappa, nerves frayed after weeks of battle, stalemates, and indecision, paced the worn grass, awaiting directions from his superiors.

Orders were finally delivered and all of Lucius's fears were made manifest. The missive directed Lucius to lead his men from behind their entrenchments, to raise their pikes and musketry against the bulwarks of Casale. The first wave of the onslaught would include his regiment, weakened by the flooded trenches that housed his soldiers, many of whom plagued by the sickness that covered several of his warriors in black boils that leaked pus and stank beyond comprehension. Grave mounds already dotted the landscape, many of the deaths were not accrued from weaponry.

When the bugles blared out the tune that signaled the moment of formation, Lucius wiped the sweat from his brow and donned the military cap fitting of his station. Mounting his steed and drawing his saber, he rallied his men into rank. The roll of the drums moved the lines forward in cadence as the defenders clambered the walls, readying black powder to defend their homeland.

THE PURPLE PISTOLLERA

The line of conflict was crossed, and the charge rushed forward as cannonry unleashed into aggressive hordes and stone fortifications. After the first volley of fire, Lucius reared his horse into place and let the initial advance run on ahead of him as he directed the second line of musketeers to aim. He miscalculated the distance, believing himself and his forces safe as enemy artillery ran closer and let loose a flurry of lead.

Lucius's horse was whittled out from beneath him as a half-dozen men fell to the devastating line of gunshot. As the wounded wailed out their pain, Lucius scurried behind the corpse of his stallion, huddling behind the fur and bleeding flesh of his trusted mount. Fortune looked down on the ranking officer who suffered nothing more than a grazing shot to the leg, still, he refused to move from his cower.

The defenders withdrew back to their ramparts, and lacking leadership, Lucius's men ran forward in a chaotic rush. In absolute shock, Officer DiCappa raised his head and risked a glance. Other flanks of the offensive have made some ground, rolling their artillery to advantageous positions. His men were far beyond earshot and too far advanced to be aided by the rest of the army. In the distance, he saw a lone, riderless horse grazing in the field. Rising to his feet, Lucius bolted for the equestrian at top speed.

PLOT TWIST

Rumor had it that Bruno skipped out of town to recuperate in the Papal States where his mother's family resided. With his gang disbanded in shame, and much of the constabulary and men of authority off to war, the Crimson Cinquedeas took full advantage to celebrate their victory. *La Tettarella del Drago* was packed to overflowing, red scarves fluttered in and out of the tavern as cheers echoed throughout the city streets.

Dolores Llorenc returned from a daring and secretive mission abroad to her apartment through a balcony window, wishing to avoid the ruckus on the ground floor, too exhausted to engage with the revelers below. She was shocked to find Lucius DiCappa rifling through her residential possessions.

"Luca?" She questioned her equally startled lover, "Why are you home so soon? The war is not over, messengers would have heralded the news ahead of your return."

He shifted about, refusing to meet her gaze, stammering for words. "I…I…" Feeling desperate and out of options, he slapped his paramour, forcefully driving her to the ground. She cupped her cheek, more wounded of heart then physically pained. He ripped her blouse and tore her silver and pearl rosary from her breast. Stuffing the necklace into a pocket and snatching a pouch from a counter, he darted out of the room.

Not long after, Jerome entered Dolores's place, "I thought I heard noises up here, was that who I think running by…" He cut short his words when he saw Dolores crying in a crumpled heap upon the floor. "*Ragazza*! What happened? This place is a disaster."

She did not respond, too absorbed in her self-pity, so Jerome shook her out of her depression. Seeing the weal on her face and torn clothing, he roared, "He did this too you! Answer me, *ragazza*!"

"He took my rosary…the only thing left from my childhood!" She sobbed, words almost unintelligible through her weeping.

"I'll kill the coward." Jerome swore through gritted teeth.

"No, Jerome!" She demanded, "Promise you won't hurt him…promise me!"

"As you say, Madame…" Jerome closed the door gently, "Not as I do." He whispered as he took to the stairs.

RESOLUTION

Lucius Bernaldo DiCappa rode his horse throughout the night, the direction did not matter, just far, far away. His transgressions were too numerous, too unforgivable, but if he could ride the distance, he could escape his sins. Leading his men to their deaths, desertion of his post, the theft and beating of his lover - he would probably have to commit more crimes along the way, it mattered little, as long as he survived.

The early dawn began to lighten the sky and Lucius dismounted from his long journey to relieve himself within a copse of trees. Afterwards, he returned to find a dark figure tying his horse to the trunk of an apricot tree.

"Reveal yourself and remove your hands from my horse!" Lucius drew his cavalry saber, directing the point at the accused.

The stranger calmly finished the knot, then quickly spun, aiming a pistol at Lucius. "You are a traitor and a thief. For this, you shall feel the edge of my blade."

He stowed the firearm into his long sash and unsheathed his broad blade, displaying a few twirls and practice slashes. Facing off with the disgraced military man, the wide saber versus the longer, more elegant horseman's blade.

Nerves shattered and at his wits end, Lucius rushed in, initiating the first attack. The defender parried the thrusts with sharp, crescent motions of his weapon. This dangerous play continued until a rider approached, interrupting the duel with a wheellock pistol at the ready and raising his voice.

"I am Jonas Villande, owner of these lands. I will have no blood shed on my orchards by two unknown vigilantes…brigands…whomever you may be."

The horseman was obviously of the landed gentry. His attire was spun of fine cloth and his mount a breed of quality. His moustache and chin beard were neatly trimmed and the grey at his temples gave him a look of distinction. The calm bearing and rationale despite the violent outbreak upon his property revealed a man of noble character and experience.

The hitherto unnamed duelist addressed the landowner in a firm proclamation, "This man I challenge is a deserter, traitor, and thief of our esteemed republic. This cur of a man has chosen his fate and I am sent to deliver justice, a military matter that transcends rights of ownership."

Lucius was panting too hard to respond, his reptilian brain in full possession as he kept attention drawn on his opponent. The lord of the land responded to the accuser, "And who are you, sir, to speak for the army? I have sons who fight in this war, so I am gravely concerned about any such occurrences referring to the matter."

"I am General Jeraldo Marke, sent by Spinola himself." The dark ruffian lied through his teeth.

Although the duelist looked more like a Barbary corsair than a military man, with his red bandana and scraggily beard, he spoke with such confidence and command that *Signore* Villande conceded. "Then I shall bear witness as a neutral observer to this accounting of justice…may the honest blade strike true."

At this point, a small gathering of farmhands and staff of the household came to view the deathmatch from afar. The duel redoubled, and Lucius's opponent could no longer toy with his prey as an audience now witnessed his affairs. He taunted the shamed DiCappa into making the first strike, and with a nonchalant riposte, the man with the eastern-styled sword rent a slash deep into Lucius's guts.

The cry of the fallen was far from noble as the victor straddled the dying man and finished his kill with a dagger thrust to the larynx. After a swift pat down, he removed a silver and pearl string of jewelry from the deceased, concealing it upon his person with a simple act of sleight of hand. Turning to the gentleman on horseback, he handed him the pouch removed from the fallen combatant.

"Use this to deliver the body to the DiCappa family. His crimes have now been addressed and your service as a second is commendable."

Jonas Villande formally asserted his consent and saluted the duelist as some of his help removed the fallen man from the estate's grounds. The lone swordsman swiped clean his broad blade upon his sash before mounting his steed for the journey back. A final farewell to the gentleman before galloping away, a dark figure riding off away from the dawning light of the rising sun.

FINALE

Ragazza, is there anything I can do to cheer you up? You have been sitting here forlorn for weeks now and you have not touched your meal."

Jerome cajoled his friend as Dolores sat dejectedly, stirring her honeyed porridge in slow, dreary motions.

"You know Jerome, I really thought he was genuine. Now I feel like I can no longer trust anyone or anything."

"Ah trust is hard won, and respect is earned with time." Realizing that his words were not helpful, he changed tact to a new course of action. "I know something that will brighten your day…let us go shopping!"

He managed to drag her out of the booth to carouse the sunny streets of Genoa. It was too early to begin drinking, so they went the routes of the seamstress shops and bazaars of the exotic goods from far off lands.

The array of dazzling colors and aromas of enticing spices did nothing to shift Dolores's frown or raise her eyes from her footsteps. Jerome tried his utmost to make enough merriment and spoofs to crack a smile, but to no avail. What did catch her attention was Jerome's awkward stumble, forcing him to the ground. Rolling to a sitting position, he pulled off one of his boots.

"Ow! Forgive me, *ragazza*. I must have a pebble in here."

She waited for her friend to dig through his footwear when her eyes suddenly grew wide as she pulled him to his feet and stormed inside a curios shop. About the neck of one of the windowfront mannequins shone the silver cross of her rosary. She jumped up and down, bombarding the seller with a barrage of questions he could not answer. Since she insisted it was hers, he sold it at the fairest of rates which Jerome demanded he pay for.

"The worthless lout must have pawned it off. If only I could have caught the bastard…" Jerome turned and winked at the shopkeeper.

For the first time in too long, he saw her smile as they departed the antiquities vendor. Dolores took Jerome by the arm and leaned against him as they strolled down the avenue. He tried not to make too much out of her touch or get too engulfed by the clean scent of her hair. He would never possess the pretty face of one such as Lucius, never have the flawless flesh of the exquisite maidens she would occasionally bed. Regardless, no one would cover her back like him, or outflank his devotion. Partners in crime till the end.

EPILOGUE

Like the first assault upon the fortified city of Casale Monferrato, the second expedition ended in disgrace, loss, and disaster for the Spanish, attempting to maintain their connection to Flanders. Through no fault of the attackers, for the island-city of Mantua had surrendered, forcing the Casale offensive to likewise desist in their superior position. The renowned General Spinola, of advanced years, died during the siege that happened to spread the horrors of the bubonic plague throughout both sides of the conflict and various principalities.

The Spanish Habsburgs, humiliated, signed the Treaties of Cherasco conceding the Mantuan territory to the French, ushering in Charles Gonzaga, Duke of Nevers, to hold sway and title over the region. The defeated fractions withdrew their forces to return in shame to their respective nations.

This coincides with the beginning of the slow decline of Genoa, quite possibly the most prosperous port-city within the great Mediterranean Sea. A renaissance republic so well-oiled that its governance often went unnoticed in the annals of history. Less than two centuries would pass before Genoa would be held by a Doge, a powerful French Emperor-General, who would himself attack Mantua and conquer much of Europe.

But that is a tale for another day…

DANSE MACABRE

well-lubricated society will often have a red-light district, an avenue for escape and indulgence, a sector where human vice can be enacted, free of judgement and prosecution. If the citizenry is stifled and repressed too harshly, the people will rise up and chaos shall ensue. But, if a civilization becomes corrupted by habituation to its lowest nature, the pendulum will swing extreme along the opposite spectrum – a precarious balance indeed.

Such insidious factors come in many forms – seductions, addiction, exploitation, forced depravity, even outright abduction and brainwashing…the list of influences is endless. Subtle or overt methods to entice the innocent or vulnerable. None were better at these tactics than the dark cult of the Demonium Cortex, purveyors of all things sinister and perfidious.

In an unholy alliance with the infernal powers, Lucivius Obitus Petitor, Hierophant Magister of the underground organization, sought to prognosticate the greatest obstacle to their ambitions. To this end, he called upon the services of Madame Noctous, the Night Woman, expert diviner of events dwelling near and far in the future. So, the blood ritual commenced, and the tall, beautifully pale woman read from the bowl of lamb's vitae in which she sprinkled leaves of nightshade and the fur of the black hare.

At the highly anticipated closure of the rite, Madame Noctous pronounced the outcome of the mechanics that enhanced the powers of her foresight.

"High Magister Lucivius, the Gods of the Dark and the Depths have spoken and have done so very clearly. The force that hinders our endeavors foremost dons the purple and wields the powder shot with no bloodshed. The singular blockage which you seek to remove is Dolores of Catalonia."

Lucivius removed his ornate headdress to itch his smoothly shorn scalp. All signs led to this conclusion, all calculations, both rational and metaphysical. Dolores, the Catalonian, was nothing more than a wee, lone woman, but she appeared to have the Fates or Angels guarding her back. Her fellowship with the Crimson Cinquedeas was an additional blockade from striking directly at the pistol-wielding maiden. Although the gang of unruly riffraff were small in numbers and political influence, the membership was quite tightknit and surprisingly skilled and wily in their undertakings. This worried the Hierophant little as he mulled over his options, for he also had a devoted and resourceful following. And the Spaniard's pure heart would make a worthy sacrifice.

****

All Saint's Day had arrived on a crisp, beautiful autumn day, a festivity for young and old alike. An annual opportunity to break caste, to dress like a king, or a monster, or a God. A brief period to swap genders, or completely obscure one's identity in masks and makeup and costumes. A holiday to bend the rules of society and let fly the freak flag of freedom ever higher.

Dolores Llorenc gallivanted about the market streets with her good friend, Jerome, as the sun sought its bedding in the west. Both wore capes and matching masks from Venice, hers purple and his, a glossy vermillion above long, stringy chin whiskers. Despite Jerome's endless misanthropic claims, he handed each child passing a smattering of candied raisins from the burlap satchel he munched from. Dolores would spontaneously burst into a string of cartwheels and back handsprings to the delight of every reveler who crossed their path. The smiles were broad and the laughter deep during this afternoon of frivolity and celebration.

A vendor offered shots of strong chianti from which the duo downed, two each before flipping coin to the seller and continuing on their merry way. The crowd thinned upon their further meanderings, and Dolores linked arms with her compadre, forcing a ferocious grin from the salty, stalwart scallywag.

Pulling Dolores into a random alleyway to escape the coastal breeze after igniting a waxed cord from a brazier, Jerome produced his short-stemmed, burlwood pipe, and layered tobacco from the West and hashish kernels from the East into the bowl, fuse-lighting the smoking contraption. The two hurled jokes back and forth at each other and rated the outfits of passerbys as rank smoke billowed from his large, hatchet of a nose.

A colorless, black and white ensemble of the Danse Macabre paraded past the narrow corridor in which the beautiful Catalonian and ugly Tuscan found themselves momentarily. They beat their timbrels and tambours in an austere rhythm that set the pace of their gothic march through the streets of Genoa. One of the skull-masked faces turned to the alley to stare ominously at Dolores and Jerome. Without missing a step, the grim-garbed witness pivoted left ninety degrees to head into the alley, followed by a train of nameless black robes, like a fanatical procession of automatons. Unnerved by the rerouting of the somber and dour band of death's celebrants, Dolores peered over her shoulder to scour a means of avoidance. At the far end of the lane, a mirror contingent of Reaper copies proceeded in their direction.

Tugging Jerome's voluminous sleeve, the Pistollera signaled with her shifting eyes the threat approaching from both sides. Nonchalantly, her gruff associate tamped out the ashen contents of his pipe and calmly pocketed the apparatus, hand near his broad-bladed dagger, wishing his trusty saber was at his side. He winked at the dusky Catalonian, acknowledging in an unspoken manner that he understood her concerns.

As the tail end of the advancing contingents continued the beating of drums, the foremost members of the Danse produced twisted daggers, snakelike blades both wicked and ceremonial. Clutching Dolores, he twirled her protectively to his rear as his offhand drew the cinquedea from his side, leering maliciously at the score of offenders who surrounded them.

The frontrunners of both flanks sped their advance to a full charge, attempting to box in the cornered rogues. Dolores looked up the building's surfaces, trying to ascertain an escape route as Jerome shifted his head back and forth, keeping his foes in perspective.

At the last moment, Jerome shifted from his defensive stance into a low, deep lunge, swiping broad with his palm-wide dagger across the torso of his nearest assailant. Sufficiently wounding the cultist, Jerome turned to blade-slap the curvilinear knife from another aggressor's grip. Meanwhile, Dolores produced her pistol from beneath her velvet cloak, quickly adjusting the flint.

Jerome's speedy left and right dives kept the fiends at bay for a time within the slim pathway until a masked fanatic from behind carved a vicious slash across the Cinquedea's tricep, forcing the Tuscan to groan through his teeth in pain and frustration. Dolores pirouetted, aiming her firearm's barrel in both directions, halting the pinching advance, and even causing the dual ranks to backpedal several paces. Shifting her weapon to the ground, she discharged her shot into the sealed latch of a grate at her feet in a thundering explosion of fetid brimstone.

"Jerome! Get us out of here!"

With his uninjured arm, Jerome heaved upon the

rusty latticework, snapping the corroded bolts from the cobblestones. Taking the lead, the nimble Dolores sprung into the small spillway, followed closely by her rugged companion. Their pursuers advanced once again, intent upon keeping their targets from escape.

"Keep your wound free of the water…you don't want it getting septic." Dolores warned.

The unlikely pair sloshed through the muck and drainage of the coastal city's underbelly with the utmost of celerity. The masked and painted faces of their followers glowed fluorescent in the dim dark of the sewers, dwindling from the fleeing couple's vision as heavy robes hampered their chase amidst the stale liquids that reeked more pungent than the foul smokes produced by Jerome's pipe.

****

Returning from brutally chastising his underlings, Lucivius Obitus Petitor entered one of the numerous chambers that made up the inner sanctum of the underworld lair. Madame Noctous reclined upon a luxurious pile of silk and satin pillows, stirring her merlot with one long finger. Her feathery lashes lifted as she gazed at the enraged cult leader.

"The next time you prophesize, give me useful information. I know my enemies, I need to know how to defeat them!" Flecks of spittle peppered his trim Vandyke beard.

"I performed exactly as you requested." The Night Woman countered, "When you are dealing with the unseen forces, you must be precise and perfectly accurate in your wording."

He pulled her up by the collar of the black robe, exposing her breasts in the process. "Don't lecture me about the nature of spirits. It is I whom holds the reins of power!" His pointed fingernails pierced small, crimson rivulets down her milk-white flesh as he grasped one of her ample bosoms.

The Night Woman did not look threatened, in fact, her expression became flushed with growing desire. She reached out with a seductive hand to drape over Lucivius's high collar. Her dark eyes obvious in their intent.

The Hierophant Magister threw her back upon the scattering of sheets and pillows, her raven locks tumbling about her exposed shoulders as he stormed out of the room. They had coupled before, but a point needed to be made. He was not going to be seduced by the night, he had to retain power and control. Furious at the lack of competence within his ranks and the simple request of removing the thorn of the Purple Pistollera from his side had yet to be achieved. Stomping to his personal chambers, he brooded upon the next phase of attaining his desired captive – the swashbuckling maiden from Catalonia.

THE STONE HEAD OF KING POLYDECTES

Fra Matteo held deep and splayed connections throughout a wide array of society's divisions and castes, with tendrils attached to the highest courts and lowliest of fences – that is why he was able to attain the services of the Purple Pistollera. Rumor held that the former man of God was an expelled member of the clergy, the scandal which led to his ousting was a well-kept secret from the general populace, not wicked enough for death, but depraved enough to have him excommunicated from a church that was responsible for genocide, rapine, and vicious imperial standards…the price paid for a lone individual questioning or acting out against decrees deemed most Righteous and Holy.

Despite the mysterious controversy, Matteo's expanse of knowledge, dredged up from the secretive recesses of the underbelly of civilization, held up in veracity impeccably. Thus, Dolores Llorenc was compelled to answer the summons of the information broker – dry but eidetic and encyclopedic of mind.

A bumbling attendant ushered her into Matteo's study, clumsy and overtly formal in his execution of duties. Fra Matteo dismissed his underling with a flick of the hand, fixated on the paperwork cluttering his hardwood desk – typical as she would come to find out. As soon as Dolores and the former monk were left alone within the library of disarray, Fra Matteo turned his full attention upon the lovely Catalonian woman, kissing her hand and cheeks gratuitously.

"Madame Llorenc, word of your heroic deeds of skill, resourcefulness, and daring have preceded your arrival with glowing praise. The descriptions of your beauty pale in accuracy now that I am graced with your presence. One that borders on the mortal and divine."

The flirtatious bookkeeper turned away from Dolores Llorenc abruptly to flip through a ledger amidst his jumble of books, scrolls, and loose sheafs of print… his one true mistress, a bibliophile of the highest caliber. The invitee, as known by those who did not know her name, called her the Purple Pistollera for her choice in garments and finery, as well as her acumen with the single-hand firearm, a skill unheard of for women of the time and domain. She studied her surroundings, having never been inside the sanctum of the intellectual who laired within the confines of the merchant-prince who currently made use of his expertise. Not from an urge to gossip or petty judgments, but out of a wholehearted and innocently curious need to understand the area in question and those who resideth within – a trait that kept her alive on more than one occasion. Matteo's library was an impressive collection of tomes, many not available to the mass of commoners. Some of the leatherbound treasures were so ancient, their handwritten script was from an age prior to the printing-press, by centuries! She turned her focus back to the archivist when he shouted out his discovery.

"*Voila, Signora*! I have found it!"

Fra Matteo produced a parchment from the chaos of paperwork and displayed the charcoal portrait of a handsome, curly-haired man with a jagged neckline. Letting her sharp eyes take in the details of the drawing, he continued, "I'm sure you are familiar with the Grecian tale of Medusa, the cursed Gorgon with the ability to turn any mortal who looked upon her into solid stone with but a flash of her gaze.

"The crafty hero, Perseus, son of Zeus and the mortal woman, Danae, was able to cut off the head of the serpent-maned Gorgon, and used her severed visage to instantaneously fossilize, if you will, the entire noble court of the Grecian isle of Seriphos amidst the Aegean Sea during the period of the early Bronze Age, before weather, war, and weakness tore apart civilization, to start anew without the help of the Gods…an Age of Man (many would say this new era was governed with mediocrity, at best – save for that rare Aurelius, or mayhaps a Caesar or Khan, regardless of the brutality utilized to maintain the concept of order). But that is a matter of polls and politics, and not of the essence of our tale, the crux and center of import, which no mathmagician has yet to discover or stumble across (save for the even more rare DaVinci or Pythagoras)."

"I have heard the story told and retold…and viewed the plays…and idled at the puppet shows." Dolores pantomimed his paradoxical ability to dramatize the tedious and banal, "But what, O' learned one, does this have to do with me being here now?" She enjoyed an adventurous yarn as much as anyone, yet she felt it best to separate her pleasures from business endeavors – lest she pilfer from her own purse, as the old saying went.

"I am attempting to be as brief as possible." Fra Matteo was taken aback by the woman's blunt manner, "I shall henceforth attempt to lead you to the heart of the matter."

Ignoring her toe-tapping, the bookish man continued his rant, "Amongst the art community, there is a myth that Polydectes, King of Seriphos island, had his head removed after its transformation to stone. How or why…I know not. Accounts differ as to the historicity and geographical destination, but the transference of dominance from the Greek to Roman empire, tells of this magnificent specimen making its way to the Papal seats, and from there, north to Tuscany, when such Pagan artifacts were threatened by the diocese.

According to rumor, the current possessor of said artifact resides not far to the east, in the commerce house of the great Medici. The statuary fragment in their possession is so exquisite that it has been the inspiration for many a renown sculptor, such as Donatello, Leonardo, Michelangelo…and most of these masters have destroyed their renditions in shame, for they could not attain the lifelike qualities captured by the mythological original. Now, the awe-inspiring piece is in the keep of the greatest sponsor of the arts…save the Church.

The former clergyman paused to catch wind, "Presently, with the decline of the Medici estates and influence, this artifact has been put on exchange in a private auction for a select few high-end bidders from the wealthiest of neighboring nations. King Louis, Rome, even the Arab nations have shown interest in this legendary purchase."

"And your patron was not worthy to match wagers with such men of pomp and esteem…do I assume too much?" Dolores smirked, lambasting the squabbles and powerplays of the decadent and their narcissistic competitions. "So, you are forced to rely on my services to procure this precious artifact, just as the highest crenulation is nothing without the bottommost cornerstone."

"Madame…" Fra Matteo interjected, "…I would never consider you amongst the dredges of society, but one step removed from the Holy Trinity. In fact, it is your unique and invaluable skill set that has drawn you to my attention."

"Speaking of value," The emboldened damsel took this opportunity to use the man's words to steer the conversation. "If I can extract this stone trinket from Florentine hands and deliver it to you, what advanced calculation can determine the risk and expense of my sacrifice? How can my priceless endeavors find a compromise in the weight of coinage? A transaction demands barter and I require a price."

****

La Tettarella del Drago was known for its seafood soup, anything goes atmosphere, and just so happened to be the gathering site of the Crimson Cinquedeas. Most fine citizens of Genoa would label this ad hoc band of scurrilous partisans nothing more than a street gang, preening and cavorting their blood-red colors and wide-bladed daggers across the portside city, but the truth was a bit more nuanced than appearances revealed. Thievery and shenanigans were a mainstay of the group's function, but this was enacted against rapscallions of a viler nature, or the well-to-do who trampled upon the unfortunate on their climb to further wealth and title.

Dolores Llorenc called a meeting of a particular member of the Cinquedeas to sup and discuss matters of future import. Sitting in a private alcove, the one known as the Purple Pistollera awaited her guest while slowly sipping on a glass of wine. She did not have to stress her patience long before a scamping, yet flamboyant presence flung the tavern doors wide to strut inside like a popinjay who owned the establishment, guffawing at the heavens.

Jerome was a specific character, with half his attire extracted from the East or the Dark Lands of Africa, like a pirate swathed in silks and sarongs of foreign territories. His straggly beard, hooked nose separating deep-set eyes, and seared skin tone made it appear like he came from such distant lands. When his seamed face glanced in the direction of the ravishing Catalonian, his laughter picked up a more joyous timbre.

"Madame Pi…Llorenc! It has been an age."

He shuffled his riding boots towards her in a fencer's advance, and when she offered her hand, he pirouetted the petite woman out of her seat before spinning her back into place like a Roma dancer. Following suit, he slid into the cubby across from her, his crimson sashes in constant motion, like a bed of striking serpents.

"Now that we have reunited after our separate excursions, I must hear everything that is noteworthy that has transpired in your adventures, my *ragazza*."

"Am I correct in recalling you telling me of being raised upon the fields of Tuscany, Jerome?" Dolores redirected the conversation, for if she let her ostentatious friend take the reins, the night would devolve into philosophical reminiscences or chaos and debauchery. She had to maintain focus on the task at hand.

"I don't remember saying such…but yes, yes. My sire oversees an orchard on the backbone of the Boot that kicks out to the sea." Jerome took the ale that was offered him by a barmaid and quaffed the heady liquid that trailed foam along his dark goat's beard. "I see not what this has to do with the here and the now, *ragazza*. Enlighten me."

"Being both a native and an artist, I am curious if you have ever visited the estates of the Medici?" Dolores questioned her best friend, looking him straight in the eyes. She knew Jerome did not like discussing his childhood, the bravo enjoyed fantasizing to others that he came out of the womb swinging upon a rope and slashing his saber back and forth. It was her job to ground his imagination, and to do so, she must capture his curiosity and sense of intrigue.

"Aye, *ragazza*. During my apprenticeship…but that

was long ago." The gruff man responded, staring into his mug as if that would clear his memory.

"And do you think you can retrieve an accurate layout of the complex? I wish to know the ins and outs of said domicile." Dolores revealed more and more while leaving the primary point obscured.

At this, Jerome's attention became piqued, "As I said, I was younger. I recollect not the exact dimensions, nor was I granted access into every room, truth be told. But get to the quick of it, Dolores, I know when you are trying to bait me like a fish to the hook. Give me the meat, *ragazza*, and do not dangle it. And leave it rare and real, as I like it."

"I carry a task, and ample reward. I offer to you a partnership for full clarity to your hawk's gaze, Jerome." Dolores looked directly at the man across from her, "Unlike any other role I have yet to attribute to you…thus, I ask of you, my most trusted of compatriots, to embark upon an expedition unlike anything relating to our previous escapades…"

"Are you here to broaden my horizons, *ragazza*?" The surly miscreant tapped out his pipe of New World tobacco ash and Eastern hashish dust upon the tavern's floor. "What is it you think I have done or not done, Madame of the Mischievous?"

"Acting!" Declared the bold instigator, "Not upon the stage or before your devoted following, but to the cynic…the unbelieving." She smirked, "Yet, tis a role all too suiting for the likes of you."

"Tell me more of said character, and I shall determine if I deem worthy to take upon myself the script for an unknown play." Scoffed the man, "Am I truly fit for the part, or is the author noteworthy enough to acquire my services?"

"Yes, my dear playwright, recruiter, and improvisational actor, you shall procure quite the accommodations for this performance." The clever protagonist prodded further her weathered coconspirator. "In fact, I cannot foresee the possibility of this endeavor coming into fruition without you."

"Truly, Dolores. You are the playwright, O Aeschylus." Jerome corrected, "Now, don't leave me hanging like Prometheus. I simply seek to know the gist of the story so I can best enact a delivery. My services are ever at your disposal…I only insist that my duties are performed to the utmost…that requires that I study my part and know the ins and outs of the scenario. I shall provide improvisations from there."

Jerome downed his tankard and slammed the glassware for emphasis.

****

All foreseeable arrangements had been settled and the precarious engagement was readied for commencement. Under Dolores's request, Jerome was asked to summon two or three of the finest climbers willing to eschew the law. Reaching throughout his broad array of contacts, Jerome sought out the most skilled of rappelling experts with a penchant for theft and criminality. To this end, the Crimson Cinquedea found Joseph McKnight and Ranaldo Tarsesse.

First came Joseph McKnight, an Irish sailor who sold his services to legit merchants and pirates alike. His many travels throughout the Mediterranean gave him cursory knowledge of the Latin tongues, though his bawdy accent remained ever present. His use of the ropes and expertise at knotwork was unsurpassed, and his longtime friendship with the gang member, both cresting middle-aged which did nothing to deter their adventurous spirits, was an added benefit of loyalty and camaraderie. Fortuitously, the boisterous Celt happened to be in the region, and Jerome enticed his old friend into their mission with the greatest of ease.

The native born Ranaldo, almost half the age of the seafarer from the Isles, made up for his lack of years with a primed young body and daredevil attitude. He made his coin repairing the domes of ecclesiastical ceilings and laying tiles upon the roofs at a bone-crushing distance above the cobbles below. Yet, during the moonlit hours, the bold Ranaldo would enjoy a healthy draught of *Drago's* homebrew and join the Crimson in defending their honor – even if that may be the honor of thieves, bastards, and the otherwise disenfranchised.

Dolores was not sure about the randy, uncouth advances of the foreign picaroon (maybe if he appeared more like his younger counterpart…). But when she learned of his successful engagement that fulfilled the first leg of their caper (a story to be told in the near future…), she hesitantly allowed the ship's rigger to accompany their menagerie (despite a not so sly attempt to joust his tongue with her own…most unchivalrous!).

During a clandestine meeting upon a flat rooftop,

beyond the reach of snoopy onlookers; Dolores, Jerome, Joseph, and Ranaldo discussed the logistics of the upcoming escapade. All proficient in the art of scaling, but the Purple Pistollera and Crimson Cinquedea would be needed elsewhere. So, they drank, supped upon game hen, and debated plans till the moon took a quarter shift in the sky and all foreseeable outcomes were hashed over thoroughly. With the date, time, and final meeting spot all situated, the foursome disbanded to secure provisions and keep distance from each other until the fateful moment came to bloom.

****

"You may find me gaudy, *ragazza*, but this is the most outrageous outfit I have ever donned." Jerome looked down at his sequined, curl-toed slippers, baggy pantaloons, jewel-stitched sash, and ornate, golden robe as he shifted his cream-colored headcloth neatly tied off by a goat-hair agal, representative of the Arab princes that wandered the desert sands of the Fertile Crescent. Extra padding was strategically placed to accentuate the paunch, with a mixture of ash and olive oil coating his beard to add grey to his features.

Dolores stifled a creeping chuckle at the sight of her friend, garbed as an Easterner. Despite the ridiculousness of the charade, Jerome looked the part without flaw. No wonder all his comrades teasingly dubbed him "the Moor."

The two had worked out their secret hand gesticulation signals – YES – NO – STOP – RUN – DISTRACT –

FIGHT! Jerome distilled his false linguistics as Dolores refined her part as half-breed interpreter for the fabled Ibn al-Muzaffar, one of the Desert Princes of Arabia. Dressed in the corset and flowing dresses of the well-to-do, Dolores Llorenc assumed her role as Aaliyah Mustafah, ambassador and middle-(wo)man between the East and West emissaries (the Orient and the Occident).

During Jerome and Joseph's preliminary excursion, Dolores, in disguise, made arrangements with the Medici household for the procurement of the auction piece. With Ferdinando II de' Medici travelling distant lands in pursuit of the latest scientific achievements, she was re-directed to the curator of the estate, one Encio Alladonde.

Well-travelled, she laid the accent on thick and pro-claimed that she was sent ahead of the great Ibn al-Muzaffar to guarantee his arrival and plan a date for the grandiose bidding. She ingratiated herself well with *Signore* Alladonde and when she asked to see the legendary piece, he was delighted to show off his master's collection.

In the vast primary hall of the museum sector, filled with paintings, sculptures, casts, and an eclectic variety of trinkets, great and small, that had been collected and sponsored throughout the centuries. It took an effort of will for Dolores to not become lost in the works of the great masters and focus on the task at hand. She reluc-tantly glanced past the carved marbles and oil or tem-pura renderings to take stock of all windows, stairwells, and doorways.

When they came to the auction piece in question, Dolores could not help but gasp at the exquisite features of the statue's severed head. Encio would not let her lift the stone, so he cradled it to let the young woman caress and adore the perfection of rendered humanity. The curls, so numerous and overlayed, seemed impossible to have been chiseled by even the finest of sculptor's tools. The slightly parted lips captured every crease and crevice of the living mouth. Even the individual, minute hairs of the eyebrows were delineated with such detail that Dolores felt a sudden sense of shame, as if she were intimately fondling a man without his consent.

Breaking from the gawking of this masterpiece, Dolores thanked the curator for granting her the privilege of a personal viewing. Over a plate of olives and aged wine directly from the family's orchards, Encio and the persona called Aaliyah finalized her return with lord in tow, three weeks' hence. Farewells were made and Dolores departed, taking coach for the sake of upholding appearances.

****

Dolores and Jerome found themselves in the high-vaulted, open-air workshop of Clayrence Lebounne, French sculptor and acquaintance of Jerome for many a year. Dolores described to the utmost of her recollection the coloration of the stone and features of the carving. She displayed the strands of clear silk that she used, most deftly, to attain the length and circumference of the statue's head. An exact copy under these time restraints was infeasible, something close was all that could be desired.

The roguish duo expressed their profound gratitude to the jovial, dirty blonde Frenchman willing to hand off his commissions to his apprentices so he could work diligently to finish their request. Dropping a purse and excusing themselves so the craftsman could get to his occupation, the twosome made their way back to their Florentine hostel, *Gli Indumenti Larghi*, courtesy of the benefactor of Fra Matteo.

Over glasses of their favorite beverages, wine and ale respectively, Dolores and Jerome mapped out what the two could make out of the broad and palatial Medici estates and enjoyed the offhand company of unknown, but convivial denizens. Dolores became inebriated enough to join in the ribald dancing while Jerome brooded over a sestina he had been inking, watching the lithe steps of the dainty Catalonian.

****

Three weeks passed swift as an arrow, and the mission was set underfoot. High noon blazed its summer rays upon the carriage bearing the impersonators of Ibn al-Muzaffar and Aaliyah Mustafah. Escorted by gallant riders past the gilt-edged portico that marked entry into the home front of the Merchant-Dukes of Florence. Riding near the stone walls of the great manor house, the two passengers spied the visages of Joseph McKnight and Ranaldo Tarsesse, garbed as laborers and busy working the manicured flowerbeds gracing the grounds beneath the southern veranda.

The coach's four horses drew to a halt at the entry

yard of the Medici. Valets led the two "foreign" dignitaries from the wagon's porch step into the cool sanctum of Tuscany's overseers. On cue, Encio Alladonde pranced down the stairs, dressed in his finest doublet of orange velvet, to greet his esteemed guests.

"*Principe* Muzaffar…*Signora* Mustafah, my apologies again for the untimely departure of my lord. But rest assured that I was granted full permission to deal fairly and legitimately with our interactions for the bid. Greetings." The curator gave the customary embrace of the region to the two guests from across the Great Sea.

"*It-shar-raf-na, wazeer. Allah Rahim abda*!" Jerome gave a slight bow to the go-between.

Dolores jumped in, attempting to cover for her partner's halted and clumsy pronunciations. "The Great Muzaffar receives your invitation with joy and the blessings of God – the All, the Merciful."

Elated, the Medici representative ushered the "Arabians" further inside to show off the fabled collection known throughout the ages and across the world.

Meanwhile, Ranaldo took the timely opportunity when the interior staff would be diverted by their heralded guests to clutch a length of hempen rope to scale the exterior walls of the structure. His Irish cohort kept a wary eye open and when a farmhand passed by, he gave a sharp shrill whistle to warn the climber visible against the sun-bleached masonry.

Joseph McKnight waved at the passerby with a toothy grin, distracting the lad from witnessing Ranaldo's ascent. The young roofer dove onto a nearby balcony ledge, lying flat on his belly, praying to the Trinity that his intrusive and unseemly actions were not beheld by anyone. Sweat rained down from his brow from a combination of the abrasive noonday sun, exertion, and nerves frayed rawer than his coarse palms and fingertips.

When the potential obstacle went upon his merry way, Ranaldo continued his scramble up the stone-facing, topping the building with the agility of a jaguar. The young roofer secured and lowered the twined cordage, allowing the audacious Celt to join his cohort, like a bandy-legged spider slinking up the web with the weighty contents of his knapsack strapped about his shoulders.

Inside the walls of the Medici villa, the Purple Pistollera and Crimson Cinquedea, in cognito, were being ushered through the opulent surroundings with great gusto from the host. Jerome luxuriated in his admiration for nostalgic views of remembered antiquity and novel exposure to newly acquired pieces. Recognizing her friend's rapture, Dolores coaxed the artistically prone ruffian from his revery.

"If we have time afterwards, *Signore*, it would be his Eminence's great pleasure to grace his falcon's gaze upon this one-of-a-kind amalgamation of rare and vintage treasures. But for the sake of priorities, for which we have crossed the desert and the sea, it would be best if we were to hold ourselves to the standard of business first and foremost, then we can rest easy taking in the sights and wonders of your household and surrounding lands."

"Very astute and pragmatic, my dear lady." Encio bowed and conceded to Dolores's rationale, "If the two of you will follow me, I shall take you both to the artifact you have traveled so far to procure."

The decorated maze of the manor was traversed until they entered the vast room that sheltered the prized Head of Polydectes. The magnificent stonework was displayed in all its grandeur for the privileged, selectively chosen audience. With beaming pride, Encio Alladonde picked up the wide-sought treasure as if it were the most holy of relics. Squinting hard with his deeply sunken eyes, Jerome examined the artifact with a professional scrutiny. Turning abruptly from his observations, the swarthy scallywag began coughing furiously into his robes.

Dolores tugged discreetly on the curator's sleeve, "*Signore*, my Lord's phlegmatic condition has been troubling him since boarding ship upon our journey here. His lungs are not adapted to the moist air of your greener lands. Would it be possible if you were to unlatch the windows in the hopes that a fresh breeze shall revive his vigor?"

"Of course…Of course." Encio hurried towards the curtained openings to unlatch the paned glass. Jerome shuffled to the nearest source of ventilation to continue his throat clearing. The mock hacking was quite convincing, his weathered lungs were well resinated with a decent layer of foreign narcotics, after all. Pulling a red silk kerchief from the folds of his attire, he began fluttering the cloth in the slight Mediterranean breeze.

While Dolores pulled Encio away to discuss the logistics of the art transaction, Jerome awaited the netted bundle being lowered to his calloused hands. Extracting the heavy yet delicate contents from the webbing, he displayed a swift, sly gesture to the petticoated Pistollera. Dolores deviously drew the curator's attention her way and his back towards Jerome who swapped the counterfeit for the original and returned to the window in another fit of racking coughs.

"I believe some material within this chamber is battling with the Muzaffar's constitution." Dolores held the curator's focus on her, "If we could retire to the lounge, we may negotiate the first transaction of the offer?"

"*Si, si*, Madame." *Signore* Alladonde rushed the guests to a more entertaining and comfortable enclosure. Over food and beverages suitable for the Muslim palate, Ibn al-Muzaffar extracted a satchel of Egyptian gold bars from his voluminous robes and handed it over to the charge of the Medici, a ten percent portion of the initial bid as a sign of good faith between merchant-princes. Departing embraces and directions were given to the location of the temporary quarters housing the Arab emissaries near the seaports of Pisa. With that, Dolores and Jerome, in disguise, departed upon the wheels of their gilded carriage.

From a small copse of wild fruit trees outside the manor grounds, Joseph and Ranaldo hopped inside the boarded wagon with the precious cargo they extracted from one of the most renown art collections the world had ever known. The four thieves passed the severed stone head about, admiring their trophy and complimenting each other's victory and particular talents.

"We did as you suggested, lass. Pristine as we got it." The Irishman drawled as he cradled the ill-gotten sculpture. "N'ver seen anything like this in all me travels."

THE PURPLE PISTOLLERA

The wily Celt carefully rolled the piece upside-down so that the jagged neckline was visible.   The broken bottom may have been the most intricate, detailed, and disturbing aspect of the specimen, as though the vertebrae and every vein had been calcified or carved out.

Ranaldo's mouth gaped at the numerous tubes and nodules coursing through the interior of the stonework. "Is the myth true? There is no way, not even the greatest artist could carve such detail and depth." Gasped the strapping, but superstitious lad.

There has been much lore and many skills lost throughout the ages…" Jerome growled low, "But who is to say, Rando? With a marvel such as this, any option is a possibility."

"One thing is certain, my fine fellows." Dolores chimed in, shedding off some of the excessive and frilly skirts, beaming her radiant smile. "Our purses and pockets shall be well padded once we are safely returned to Genoa."

*****

The Arabian caravel, *Il Fawl Kalonya*, had its hull rent by a brilliant and deafening black powder explosion some nights previous. The damage was not severe enough to sink the anchored vessel, but the commotion brought the attention of the authorities.

Centuries old tensions between the Mohammedans and Christians heightened the already precarious situation, so the crew and all passengers of the ship were quarantined aboard until further investigations deduced the cause and culprits of the incendiary incident. This setback greatly infuriated the actual Ibn al-Muzaffar, imprisoned upon the damaged vessel, treated like a prisoner after being invited as an esteemed guest of the inland Medici. After nearly a week, the only clue the constabulary discovered came from a drunken stevedore claiming he witnessed two weathered and salty pirates departing *Il Fawl Kalonya* by rowboat in the dark of the night before the disastrous fireworks display.

When Ibn al-Muzaffar finally made his way into Florence, his fury grew to new heights as he learned from a flustered Encio Alladonde that the fabled Head of Polydectes was swapped for an impostor piece. The Desert Prince demanded compensation for his insufferable and fruitless journey before storming off, cursing the deceit of the Europeans and promising revenge from Mohamed's holy jihadists.

Ferdinando, the second of his name, eventually returned to his villa only to be informed of the burglary of one of the central and most mysterious items of the family collection. Being a man of reason and despiser of superstition, but also a soul whose fate placed him in the inherited position to maintain and uphold his family's estate and pride, Ferdinando thought it best to cancel the bidding war and pull a cover over the embarrassing situation.

Unfortunately, poor Encio Alladonde became the one held responsible for allowing the theft to occur from the Medici Museum during his watch. Thus, he was solemnly terminated from his duties as auctioneer and dismissed from the household in shame. Fortunately, some secret, unnamed sponsor put in a good word for the curator to the Holy Roman Church. So, he promptly relocated to Rome, the seat of the Papal States, and resumed his career for the theocracy (ever willing to compete for primacy in the shifting realms of economics and artistic grandeur).

And hence, the disappearance of King Polydectes's severed head became lost to the annals of history.

****

Dolores Llorenc, gingerly yet with a flourish, unveiled her abducted trophy from the protective confines of its velveteen casing. Fra Matteo cast his diligent gaze upon the object before pushing a hefty satchel clinking with precious coins across the table.

"Your reputation is well earned, Madame. My benefactor shall be most pleased by the timely and secure procurement of this acquisition."

"And my crew will be greatly satisfied with this compensation." Dolores tied off the cords to the oversized purse, then looked squarely at the broker, hands on her hips. "But I am curious, and after risking my neck for the noose, feel I have the right to ask this…What is your employer's interest in such a piece? Many do not believe the fantastic tale of this sculpture's origin, so the price for the object seems extremely variable depending on the purchaser. And now the ability to put this on the open market is hindered by the fact that it is currently an illicit good. So, once again, the customer pool becomes increasingly smaller and smaller, which makes me ascertain that a previous deal has been worked out."

Sighing, Matteo's shoulders slumped as he addressed the bold, brilliant, and beautiful larcenist. "I make it a habit of not normally revealing my sources, and do not typically divulge the motivations of my host…but I feel you should know the future of your acquisition for it may ease your conscience.

"The final resting place for the Head of King Polydectes will be amongst the Grecian nations. The head is returning home." The ex-monk said with dramatic finality.

Dolores appeared confused, "But are not the lands of the Greeks held by the Ottomans?"

"Not all." Matteo corrected the Catalonian, "Both Genoa and Venice hold sway over several of the islands that dot the Aegean. This shall be a gesture of good will and help to form a greater alliance in order to keep the advancement of the Moors at bay. For if the entirety of the Greek lands were to fall, it would not be long until the Muslims were at our doorsteps."

"Dolores nodded, satisfied with Fra Matteo's response. "I bear no ill will for the Muslims, but I would prefer if Genoa remained as is. A home of wonder worth defending."

****

At a private booth in *La Tettarella del Drago*, Dolores slid coinage into the grasping hands of Joseph, Ranaldo, and Jerome. The young Ranaldo thanked Dolores profusely and rushed to the bar to begin the process of lightening his load. Joseph split his stack in half and cocked a brow at the ravishing Spaniard who arranged and financed their latest caper.

"I would take a fifty percent cut if I could spend the rest of me stay in the lassie's chambers."

Dolores pulled back in unconcealed disgust from the gropes of the lewd Irishman, "I am no lady of the night, not even an expensive one. But I shall forgive your slight to my honor and standards since you performed so valiantly and vitally during our resplendent quest, and out of respect for your friendship with Jerome, who manages to overlook your viper persona."

Joseph McKnight feigned a broken heart with the pouting face of a child trying to guilt his mother into forfeiting just one more sweet roll. Jerome interrupted Joseph's sham theatrics with a stiff elbow to the ribs.

"I'm afraid to admit that there are other dark-lidded, dusky, voluptuous beauties that will unfortunately allow you to run your gropy, briny fingers over their smooth flesh." Jerome continued to prod Joseph until the frisky Celt was forced from the bench to his feet. "Try your Irish luck elsewhere, *amico*. Myself and your failed attempt at a paramour have much to discuss, and your penchant for gossip crosses borders. I do not wish for loose legs to pry open your loose lips."

Joseph swiped his pointy cap up and a handful of his coin pile from the hardwood table before enacting an exaggerated bow to the woman many deemed the most enticing within the establishment. "Well then…I shall take my robbings from the rich to disperse among the poor. And when you are in need of this merry man…you know how to find me, bonnie lass."

With a wink and a pirouette, the bawdy sailor entered the revelry, brushing against the bosoms of dancing tavern wenches and slapping the buttocks of male and female alike. Chuckling, Jerome turned from the spectacle to matters more intricate.

"Forgive him, *ragazza*, for he knows not what he does. He comes from another land and is not fully acclimated with our more chivalrous culture. Although I consider Jo Jo a most trusted compatriot, do not judge me…fully…by my company." Jerome took a long gulp from his dwindling tankard, awaiting Dolores's response with his beady eyes.

"Ha! Do not play act so innocent, Jerome. It is unseemly of even you to steal lines from the Good Book to make excuses and shift blame to one so intimate with your endeavors." She lowered her enormous cavalier's hat over Joseph's remaining payment, the wide brim swallowing half the table.

"I may be rough around the edges, Madame Pistollera. But even a scoundrel such as I have more couth than that lout. Come now, *ragazza*…my imperfections can be outdone as you have just witnessed." He answered in such a way that Dolores was not sure if her partner was joking or serious (or both).

"That is not saying much…Moor." Dolores abruptly stopped herself from continuing along these lines, looking down in shame. "Apologies, Jerome. You did not deserve such a jibe."

"What ails you, my pretty Pistollera? We should be celebrating, not dwelling in gloom and undeserved despair." Jerome reached across the table to take hold of her hand, his touch more tender than his harsh demeanor and rough callouses could possibly seem to convey… yet…

She broke composure with her friend's uncharacteristic vulnerability, a shared moment of inexplicable and raw connection. "What is it that we do, Jerome? Do we endanger ourselves and others? For what exactly? I truly wish no harm on anyone. Yet, I find my talents leading me to a dark and unholy outcome over and over again."

"A bit of both, of course. We walk one foot in light and one in shadow. It is your true heart that keeps us on course." Then Jerome broke into a savage grin, "But you cannot deny the thrill of the chase and the escape, the fight and the victory. And regardless of your despondency, I can still see the glint in your eye." The rogue smirked, "The liveliness generated from our covert, yet gallant ventures are irresistible and undeniable.

"And fret not your Christian soul, *ragazza*." Jerome proceeded onward, catching the indecision in her expression. "You are the heroine in this story of our times. A modern Perseus, no mewling Andromeda. Guided by wise Athena and clever, tricksy Hermes…yet tempered by your self-sacrificing Christos. By your own account, the treasure we recovered at our own risk has been absconded by one thieving hand to another. Yet you returned it to its place of origin. Means to a greater end, as they say…"

The smile that cracked her exquisite features revealed her concession to Jerome's over the top explanation. "Jerome…you make me blush as red as the outlandish cloth you use to contain your Medusa curls." She withdrew her hand to down the rest of her beverage.

Her rugged cohort looked down at his own empty mug before swiping a coin from Joseph's remaining scatterings. "Well…our first round has been depleted, what do you desire for the second, Madame?"

She pulled a coin from her own purse to replace that of the Irishman. "A vintage…sharp as your saber, complex as my conundrum, deep as our bond…and purple in hue."

THE DOG LOCK

ack so soon?" The gruff jibe growled from the bowels of the smithy. Singed mineral oil and the tang of carbon smoke gave the question a demonic, authoritarian overtone.

"You should be more appreciative towards a returning client, Giovanni." The softer, more subtle voice managed to cut above the coal-fueled flames and sharp hisses of cooling metal. Her supple leather boots high-stepped the tangled array of cables, ventilation tubing, and discarded scraps of raw iron.

Giovanni rubbed soot onto his razor-shorn head and turned from his work to address the slight, dark-clad figure. "I finished your request, on schedule as duty demands."

The enormous brim of the gaudy cavalier hat that concealed her face, turned to follow the brawny smith to a large safe where he produced a hand-held item wrapped in oilcloth. He pivots back to reveal the contents to the purchaser with pride.

"Based off a Northern design but given an Italian flare."

The musket's proportions were exquisite, near perfection. The metallic casings hugged the cylindrical frame like a lover. The polished hardwood gleamed in harmony with the brass and steel. Even the handle was planed finely enough to balance comfortably inside her delicate grip as she examined the craftsmanship. The smith's charred fingers pointed to the intricate workings of the cocking mechanism, shaped in the manner of a howling beast.

"This, this is what makes the pistol unique. The joining of the pan and lock provide a safer, more sure shot."

As the burly-armed blacksmith turned to grab a receipt, the woman garbed as an adventurer deftly removed her offhand from a side-pocket to better caress the firearm. She timed her manipulations with the rhythm of the boiler-powered bellows that replaced the need for an apprentice. Illicit endeavors demanded a need to work in secrecy.

"The materials, design, and effort are all in order." He handed the tally over, "But the act of me sacrificing my livelihood to sale armaments unlawfully into the hands of a woman shall require a doubling of the total cost. You do understand our position?"

With a sudden punch, she plunged the barrel firmly around an inset wall tong and swiveled the sight upon the forger's hulking torso.

"I shall pay a man's price for a man's weapon!"

Giovanni's heavy brows scowled as he reached for a hammer, but she tapped the dog lock in warning.

"Unbeknownst to you, I capped and loaded your beautiful implement, *Signore*." She redirected the gun towards the elaborate boiler system that regulated the temperatures of the furnace. "Negotiations are in my hands."

The man's eyes grew wide at the threatening gesture, "Are you mad? Destroy that and you kill us both!"

"A swifter punishment than I shall receive if caught with this." She set a purse upon the bill and an extra coin, "Full payment, and a lira for the artisanal touch."

He grumbled but nodded his reluctant consent as she backtracked the metallic maze. Her shadowy cape unfurled as she vanished into the Genoese streets.

JASIAH WITKOFSKY
JASIAH WITKOFSKY

DOUBLE CROSS
TRIPLE TAKE

She was not claustrophobic or afraid of the dark, nonetheless, this was most definitely an uncomfortable predicament. Dolores Llorenc reluctantly allowed the men escorting her to pull a bag over her head to meet her potential employers at a secret location. But Dolores was the Purple Pistollera and she did not earn that title without a clever mind, so she had her compatriot, Jerome, follow from a distance.

Blinded and guided into a horse-drawn carriage, she took a seat across from one of her deliverers and felt the cart lurch into motion. Breathing slow to calm her racing heart, she shut her useless eyes to allow other sensations an opportunity to take primacy.

Counting her heartbeats, she estimated the journey was not far distant from their meeting point, less than half a league distant. Her fellow passenger gently took her hand and led her out of the cart, where she heard a door unlatch. Stepping downward, she determined the destination in which she headed lay underground in some basement or cellar. Another door opened and the sound of many voices sent a cacophony to her ears before the blinding hood was removed from Dolores's striking features.

The room was packed with a variety of unsavory scoundrels, bar wenches, brutes, connivers, and sea bandits from around the globe. The smokes of a multitude of intoxicants hazed the upper half of the crowded, dimly lit chamber, wine and liqueurs flowing freely. At the far end of a large oak table sat two identical women eyeing the newly arrived Dolores, one of which opened her painted lips to address the Pistollera.

"Take a seat, *Senorita*. You grace our presence with much anticipated pleasure."

Dolores rested her posterior upon a chair near the mirrored sisters and attempted to differentiate the two. The gorgeous siblings shared the obvious Spanish characteristics with the Pistollera, dark of hair and bronze complected. Both women were petite in stature but sat taller than Dolores by a finger's width. She guessed their ages surpassed her own by less than a decade, middle aged but still in their prime. Both shared a sinister and seductive gaze between hoop-pierced ears. They donned matching red and black, puff-and-slashed tunics and crimson scarves kept their raven tresses from obscuring their vision. Tattooed upon the inner flesh of their right forearms, the imprint of blood-drenched daggers. Their left arms bore separate halves of a split heart, the most discernable difference between the two.

The speaker introduced themselves, welcoming

their oddly procured guest. "Greetings Lady Llorenc of Catalonia, I am Juna, and this is my sister Maya, fortuitously born between the cusps of the two months, never separated by more than an arm's length." She clapped her sister's back in the spirit of camaraderie, "We are the Toledo Twins, and we are overjoyed to meet the Girluerra of Genoa, as you are known to the west. Pour the dear lass a drink, Havi."

A bald, muscle-bound giant of a man delicately poured Dolores wine from an enormous ceramic jug as she responded. "I would not call myself a warrior, but I am a woman of means and well-connected, truth be told."

Juna laughed heartily, "Ah, so modest. We have heard differently…and that is why we have sought out your services. So let me get to the heart of the matter of your summons." The outlaw spokeswoman downed a draft before continuing.

"As you may have ascertained, we are newcomers to this fair city, but we have a dire purpose to enter the confines of this here port. A matter of birthright pride and a desire to balance the scales of justice which we assume you can relate to."

The verbose half of the matching sisters continued her recital, hitting ever closer to the heart of the situation that brought the Catalonian transplant to the presence of the twins from Toledo, the City of Three Cultures, two regions aligned under the greater, overarching banner of the Spanish Empire. "Our precious gold, extracted from Nueva Espana, has been redirected to the misfortune of our own great peninsula and its fine citizenry, to the beneficiaries of our most generous efforts who have snubbed our sacrifices by refusal to acknowledging our loans with any form of payment whatsoever. Thus, they line their coffers with our hard work and offer nothing in return. We merely seek to recorrect this egregious imbalance after years of slights, thefts, and wrongdoings, despite all our most trusting gestures of goodwill. So…we desire to redress this grievance in the most subtle and ephemeral manner possible. And that is why we have conscripted your most invaluable skills. You, Dolores Llorenc, who straddles both worlds, could assist our great kingdom like no other."

"So, you two represent our great nation?" Dolores challenged, wary as to why such unsavory characters would play off the role of noble ambassadors. "I would be most remiss if I were to assume such a standing and title with nothing more than the happenstance of my land of rearing."

Maya, the silent sister, unmoved until now, extracted a golden seal from her blouse and slammed it down upon the sturdy oaken wood table to emphasize their authority. To add credence to the physical evidence produced to assuage the astute and rigid sensibilities of the Pistollera, the vocal twin bent low to Dolores's ear and whispered a confession for her ears alone.

"If I may trust you with a secret, my sister and myself are undercover actors for the throne of Castille and Aragon. Molded and trained to infiltrate the underbelly and outreaches of Spain's neighboring allies and antagonists."

Juna slinked back to her seat, allowing Dolores to

ruminate over the multi-armed bundle of information thrown into the Pistollera's lap. Amidst the den of the unknown, inside the belly of the beast, Dolores processed the couched hints, scandalous posturing, and desperate need for her assistance. Sipping off her glass carefully, she set the chalice down and slid it forward, tilting her head towards the talkative twin with her eyes on both.

"To the point then. What makes you assume I have any capacity to aid you in your endeavors? So far, I have been labeled a warrior and more, but I desire specifics. For after all this blather, I have yet to determine the true purpose of my summons." Dolores opined, "So, if you were to be so generous, kindly spit out your proposition and allow me to mull over your scheme as entailed by a proper and decent business arrangement."

Juna chuckled, impressed and satisfied by the moxie and clear boldness of the Pistollera's response, forcing her to delve into the true heart of the matter. "We need you to infiltrate the Church of Santa Domingo to procure the ill-begotten gold and gems procured rightfully by the Empire of Espana."

"So…" Dolores tickled her chin thoughtfully, "You wish to send me as an invader into the House of the most Holy, to the defiance of God Himself, to procure what exactly for you? Conquered gold stolen from some hapless tribes. If I am to fight, it shall be for the cause of righteousness and the underdog, not for the greatest global power known to man."

"What has taken place years before our births matters little to current events and cannot be altered by the likes of us." The talkative twin from Toledo countered attempting another tactic to entice Dolores to her machinations. "What matters now is to redress the injustices dealt out upon the living. And in that goal, we require your invaluable assistance."

"And if I were to give credence to that sentiment, what incentive do I have to burglarize a church. Mind you, I hold in high esteem any who have devoted their lives in service to the Trinity." Dolores invoked a religious rebuttal.

"Bah! Don't be so naïve." Juna retorted, "Even one as devout as yourself must understand that the Church does not only house the holy, but some of the most vile, loathsome villains are involved within the organization…you know this at heart if you refuse the blatant truth granted to you by your eyes and ears.

"Fra Benuardo, the head of Santa Domingo, was granted a loan from the Spanish clergy to bolster his sanctum in the hopes to forge stronger bonds with the separate states that form the chain between Spain and the Papal States. Since that time, nearly a decade past, Benuardo has used the generosity of our homeland to partake in the child slave exchange and lined his own pockets with no sign of ever repaying his debts. This man's sins are beyond count, and he needs to be taken down, whether it be to rot behind bars or felled by the blade."

"I am not the combatant you think me, for I will not kill another, no matter how loathsome." Dolores stated her limitations with clarity, "But if what you say about this clergyman is true, which I shall uncover, then I will suffer no regrets to witness his downfall."

"There is more." Juna continued with a heavy arch of one eyebrow, "Whatever wealth extracted shall be split three ways between us, Spain does not mind rewarding its allies. Any provisions needed for your mission, we should be able to procure for you in a timely fashion."

Dolores quaffed the last of her glass and waved off Havi who attempted to refill her cup. "Then I shall meet you at *La Tettarella del Drago* Monday, the day after the Sabbath, to determine what I shall uncover, and to give you your final answer about the feasibility of your scheme."

"No." Juna laced her tone with practiced authority. "We will meet at the market-port, our position here cannot be compromised." The twin had to have the final word on the exchange, not wanting the Catalonian to hold any home turf advantage as she waved her escorts forward.

The Pistollera snatched the hood out of one of the men's hands, covering her own face to retain what dignity she could from the situation. "And when I return here successful, I will not come masked, for I will have most certainly earned that trust."

****

Dolores knelt at the foremost pew in her finest black dress, face concealed by a lady's brimmed hat and veil, looking much the part of a grieving widow. After the sermon, the vast majority of the attendees had departed the Church of Santa Domingo upon this Sabbath to feast and spend the remainder of the day with family and good company.

With the clearing of the temple of God, Dolores was better able to evaluate the trappings decorating the interior as Jerome entered the confessional. The walls, once peeling and decrepit, had been newly replastered. While there was no fault in restoring a decaying structure, the stained-glass windows edged in copper and glistening with gems denoted opulence and undue extravagance. The object that caught her attention was the large cruciform mounted above the dais, a cross of solid gold filigreed with bands of silver, centered and surmounted with beautifully chiseled emeralds. A symbol of luxuriance so gaudy that it was surprising that Christ had not arisen once more to expel the moneylenders.

The woman whom many called the Purple Pistollera recited her prayers and read more Scripture to memory before Jerome returned from the confessional booth scratching at his freshly trimmed beard Dolores forcefully cleaved into his face. Linking elbows, Jerome led his young, beautiful companion from the house of worship to the light of the pleasant Genoese sun.

"What did you discover, my half-shorn Moor?" Dolores teased her friend, admirer, and protector. "Is our dear Fra Benuardo plump with pilfering or peasant's pie?"

"The man is filth and should be eradicated from existence!" Jerome spat in a heated whisper. "I fed him some tripe about defiling children and male orgies." Dolores's friend sneered, "I could hear him panting inside and smell his sweat. Guilty as charged, says I!"

Dolores shushed her compatriot with a finger crossing her lips, looking back discreetly through her veil to see if they had been overheard. At the far end, upon the dais, the piggish Fra Benuardo was wringing his hands in apparent delight, precious metals and exotic stones banding each of his swollen fingers. Halting Jerome at the collection bowl, Dolores made a show of tribute, opening her purse and depositing alms to balance the scales for actions to come.

****

The Pistollera confirmed her acceptance for the Toledo-hatched caper with a finality that surprised even herself. Juna and Maya financed the tailor to custom fit a nun's habit for Dolores's tiny yet athletic frame. Her childhood spent in a convent allowed her a well-practiced disguise as Sister Diana from the Halls of the Virgin Maria, sent from Espana to catalogue finances and collect accrued debts. A missive was sent to Santa Domingo by the fictional Sister arriving from Toledo to elicit a private meeting with the church's head to discuss a monetary exchange rate.

Dolores sent scouts from amongst the Crimson Cinquedea gang to intercept the return message exiting the Santa Domingo. From there, all that remained was for the Pistollera to wait patiently to enact the second part of the mission.

The return letter took less than a week to reach Dolores's hands, notifying her that Fra Benuardo would be willing to host Sister Diana upon the last Sunday of the month after confession, giving her less than a fortnight to plan for the day she would introduce her newest alter ego to the corpulent clergyman.

Infiltrating Santa Domingo with the most innocent and religious of the Cinquedeas, the wily Pistollera continued to have the priest followed, inside and out of the church. A revolving shift of spies allowed her to stay intimately informed with the habits and whereabouts of her mark, and the hours in which his occupation transferred to the realm of the personal. When not consorting with her cohorts, Dolores tidied up on her Scripture and devised further depth and backstory for the role she was soon to enact.

Laying low and doing her utmost to keep her more rowdy associates focused and sober, Dolores conferred with Jerome in the bowels of *La Tettarella del Drago* for a counterplan if all else failed. The intricacies of her situation brought upon an incessant nagging between the thin line of morality she constantly toed, and her chronic need for the thrill of adventure and mischief. Caught between the patriotic prods of her homeland and the ethical insinuations of the Church, neither of which remained free of guilt and criticism, Dolores unloaded her reservations to the critical examinations of Jerome's twisted and open mind. That is why she valued her favorite companion most highly, she provided the moral conundrum, but he would incessantly urge her on to finality and action – a stalwart push to execution.

****

The final Sunday of the month brought the warbling

of songbirds heralding a faint smattering of clouds gentling the rays of the bright Mediterranean sun. Donning her habit and utilizing her makeup not to accentuate, but age, Dolores Llorenc descended from her room at *La Tettarella del Drago* to arouse her posse.

Jerome was already seated at the dining hall in his favorite alcove, smearing toast with hen's eggs as he guzzled watered wine. Turning to his friend disguised as a nun, he raised a bushy eyebrow, "Your new dress fits you splendidly, *ragazza*." The bawdy jokester eyed the beautiful Catalonian up and down.

"You should be taking this situation as seriously as a monk, Moor." Dolores rolled her eyes, taking a seat across from her boisterous associate. "Speaking of, where are your robes? You are supposed to be prepared to back me up."

Pulling a dark, crumpled pile of coarse cloth from beneath his rear, Jerome flashed a gleam from his beady eyes. "As always. I am five steps ahead of you, Madame Pistollera. And unlike you, I shall slip it on at a more appropriate time." Jerome was in a jovial mood, typical for one who reveled in the thrill of the hunt and the chase.

The rest of their cohorts joined the duo, one by one until all the conspirators stood present. Donning the hooded monks' robes supplied by the twin agents from Toledo, concealing and securing what weaponry or tools they could beneath the heavy fabrics during their final moments of deliberation. From a dingy alley, a procession of a dozen cowled monks, six before and six behind, led a dainty nun through the Genoese streets – a dramatic reenactment to assume solemn roles.

Reciting prayers in a harmonized chant, Jerome broke from his acting to hiss in Dolores's ear. "Yer skirts would look best if they were cut to the thigh…maybe remove the midriff."

Dolores whispered low, "So help me God, I will remove your man-parts with my stiletto."

The religious train reached the open double doors of the Church of Santa Domingo and entered the pristine white walls of the refurbished House of the Lord. The piggish priest, Fra Benuardo, was leading a stout and obviously wealthy matron from the confessional box with his arm about her, chumming up the bejeweled sponsor with a sickening grovel. The clergyman's multiple chins quivered with anticipation as the woman left a sizable deposit in the offering basket.

"Father, the Sister Diana is here from Toledo, as ordained." Guiseppe, the spokesman, interrupted the officiant as he was fervently emptying out the coins and trinkets given by the congregants of the day's mass. "We come on the day and the hour of your suggestion."

Hhhm? Oh, yes. Sister Diana from the House of the vestal Madre Maria, an honor to finally meet one who has traveled so long. I hope your journey was pleasant and you find beautiful Genoa to your likings. Come, let us discuss matters in my office. Your retainers may make use of the church and eat of our loaves."

As soon as the doors to the inner rectory were heard to be shut, the dozen 'monks' sprung into action. Muffling the clergy and altar boys, several of the Crimson Cinquedeas unwound the ropes that corded their waists to bind their hapless captives before gagging them and stuffing them into the dark confines of the confessional. Men fastened their staffs together as Jerome motioned half of his crew further into the bowels of the church to scour the halls for other followers and any wealth to be procured.

Bending a copper candlestick and attaching it to the assembled pole, Jerome stepped upon the shoulders of two of his cronies, being the smallest, and was hoisted high upon the tall chapel wall. A couple of rogues finished barring the entrance doors as Jerome fished with his extended rod to remove the mounted cross of gold and gems, the focal point of the church.

Finagling the long and awkward implement, Jerome miscalculated the weight of the golden religious symbol as it dislodged from the plaster to tumble disastrously to the stone floor. Jerome held his tongue, cursing his luck, but unleashed a sigh of relief when a teammate spotting his precarious position dove forward and caught the precious artifact in the folds of his robe.

Meanwhile, Dolores, in the role of Sister Diana, took a seat opposite the church's head, taking inventory of her surroundings from between heavy lashes. Fra Benuardo brought out a crystal carafe and poured each of them a glass of sweet red wine. The false nun wished to remain sober to maintain the sharpness of her faculties but figured a little bit of relaxation might help ease her nerves during the demanding ordeal she had found herself in due to her own machinations.

The Fra attempted to engage his guest with a blathering of small talk, possibly to distract her from the reason for her visit, but Dolores played the role of the curt no-nonsense nun solely here for business – drawing from the vast experience of her childhood under the tutelage of demanding Sisters within the orphanage of the Virgin. Sighing, the overweight priest bent over to extract pamphlets of papers from a cubby within his desk.

Handing over a fistful of receipts, Dolores scrolled through the tedious collection of numbers signifying costs spent for the reconstruction of the church and expenses necessary to maintain its sacred services. Although she was no mathematician, her quick mind could make out that the totals did not add up with the amount rattled off by the women from Toledo. Asking for a sheaf and quill, Dolores quickly penned some notes, deciding on the tact necessary to deal with this hustler.

"Everything here appears legit, and your organization of dates is truly commendable." She flattered the obese and sweating man, his beaming smile proving that he was prone to compliments. "Still, this does not account for the entirety of the funds loaned to you."

"Well…" the man stumbled for words, "Some finances have been stored as a fallback for any future disasters. Running a congregation is not performed by faith alone."

"Tis true. But have you not been making compensations through donations and the charity of your flock?" She kept her eyes firm upon his shifting pupils. "I full well understand that a church must be maintained. But you must have wealthy patrons, like the woman who departed as we entered…and despite the severity of what I must say next, you do owe much to the Empire of Spain and you have yet to fulfill your loans. And if you can't maintain your seat, we will be forced to take our complaints to Rome itself"

Benuardo's balding scalp was now beading with sweat as his thick neck grew red. Excusing himself, he settled his bulk before a cast iron safe, unlocking the hinged opening and producing a satchel that sang with coin. Turning back to Sister Diana, he set the bag upon the center of the desk.

"This is the grand majority of our savings. Five hundred liras should be contained inside, in the hopes it will suffice until next year when we have accumulated more finances. Please! Take it all. I implore you." The piggish man groveled pathetically.

Dolores briefly rifled through the shining contents of the satchel when a dull set of raps reverberated from the other side of the door. Fra Benuardo shifted his massive bulk to answer the summons, cracking the door slightly to greet the knocker. Dolores could not discern any distinct vocabulary from the doorway murmurs, but the fact that members of the clergy were still around to converse with the priest concerned her greatly.

The hulking clergyman closed the door gently and slowly turned back to his seated guest, wiping the swamp of his brow. Inhaling a deep breath, Fra Benuardo dropped into his seat and squinted his beady eyes at the nun before him.

"It has come to my attention that the men who have accompanied you, Sister Diana, have captured my underlings and infiltrated the inner recesses of my church. Before you leave that chair, I must find out what exactly is going on." To emphasize his point, he reached down and grabbed a club lined with small pyramids of iron, setting the weapon upon the desk in front of him.

From the depth of her voluminous sleeves, Dolores produced with lightning celerity her dog lock pistol, aimed straight towards the heart of the stout man in the white and gold robes of the preacher. Without batting a lash, she cocked the hammer with her free hand, leveling the barrel above the snout of the astonished priest.

"I was warned of your excessive greed and corruption, so I came prepared. I hold all the cards here and it will do you no good to bash in the head of a nun."

Fra Benuardo sweat profusely enough to rain salty drops upon the wooden handle of his mace. Nonetheless, the shaken, pudding bowl of a man held what power he could muster, out of desperation if nothing else. "One of your followers is now in our custody… a youngling caught snooping in my personal chambers. If you care for his life, you will lower your pistol, Madame."

Bolting to her feet and spilling her chair to the floor, Dolores pressed her firearm to the creased forehead of the churchman, the stench of fear infiltrating her delicate nostrils.

"If any of my company is harmed, you will not survive the day!" Keeping the gun jammed into his skull, Dolores tore the man's gaudy crucifix from the clammy folds of his neck. "This I swear to you by the Lord Above!"

"I die, he dies… and you will not set foot outside of Genoa." Fra Benuardo stammered, sputtering out any words that would save his standing and blubbering hide.

Dolores swiped the studded cudgel from the tabletop, shattering the bluff of the rotund coward who could no longer obfuscate his veneer as bully and holy man. Snarling down at the sluggish-skinned man with one foot upon the desk, she expelled out her demands, clear and forceful. "You call your men and have them retrieve your captive! If any blood or tears are shed, I will burn your church to the ground!" She clutched the stolen crucifix tightly, hoping she sounded serious. "And I saw another sack in your safe box. Debts must be paid!"

The youthful Siero was returned to his fellow Cinquedeas, and the band of rogues departed swiftly by way of the back exit. Stripping off their cumbersome robes as they fled into the dusk-lit avenues of the port-city, the Pistollera cut a slit down the length of her gown with her stiletto to allow her legs a wider range of movement.

When the thirteen infiltrators felt they had safely evaded the vicinity of Santa Domingo, they slowed pace to catch their breaths and cheer a successful raid. Jerome growled playfully at Dolores's exposed leg revealed through the rent in her robes.

Now you have it, *ragazza*. The right set of boots and you have quite the outfit there."

"Jerome!" Dolores was not in a playful mood, "That situation we barely escaped could have easily turned into a failure. Your negligence compromised Siero's life, and that fat monk was willing to club my brains out my ear." Her frustration war apparent in the long strides of her short legs.

"Tis true. I did not think to explore the catacombs. A severe mishap on my part." Jerome admitted his lapse in calculations which could have ruined their mission. "But I'll make it up to him back at *del Drago*, isn't that right Siero?" He pulled the young man to his side with his arm about his neck as he swatted Dolores's curvilinear derriere.

Without looking back or missing a step, the Pistollera backhanded Jerome hard across the face to the hearty guffaws of his fellow Cinquedeas. Rubbing his cheek and chin, the swarthy scoundrel grinned broadly at the back of the Madame's head.

****

Dolores Llorenc stepped into the carriage with a stuffed handbag in each arm and a large satchel strapped to her side, this journey no hood was drawn over her exquisite features. She took note of the route the four horses transported her across even though she knew exactly where she was going. The guardsman sitting across from her did not utter a peep, which suited the young woman just fine as she likewise held her tongue, the clop of hooves echoing throughout the lonely night.

The sneakthief was carefully delivered to a row of warehouses and shop stalls that lined the seaside. The driver and escort protectively led Dolores between them to a narrow break separating buildings to a worn and inconspicuous doorway. A series of keys revealed a stairway leading downward that Dolores last traversed blindfolded. Clutching her packages securely, she descended the dim and creaking interior betwixt the two taciturn coachmen.

THE PURPLE PISTOLLERA

The raucous and smoky atmosphere of the under-lair mirrored Dolores's previous visit some weeks prior with the wild array of exotic characters and heady intoxicants – opioid hues, hashish billows, and alcohol fumes. The Pistollera took one final whiff of sanity before entering the chaos of the tunnel-dwelling, criminal class, the undesirable dregs who scraped the bottom and vanished with little or no trace.

The diminutive beauty was offered a seat at the grand table where she gratefully deposited the heavy contents of her luggage upon the weathered surface of the milled boards of aged oak. Defiantly eyeing the surrounding swarm of miscreants to brand her place amongst the riff-raff, Dolores caught the displacement of a curtained divide revealing the striking presence of the Toledo Twins – Maya and Juna.

Taking their accustomed seating arrangements at the head of the grandiose table, the identical sisters smiled voraciously towards the lone woman cloaked in deep purple who offloaded her stash of reapportioned riches. Grinning back at the dual daughters of Toledo, Dolores boldly took a seat, radiating a fearless aura behind her sacks of booty amidst a gathering of questionable ruffians. With all the bravado of a fox in an unmanned chicken coop, Dolores kicked her booted feet upon the beaten tabletop and reclined back on the hind legs of her chair.

"I see you have come back to us successful in your endeavors, I knew you were the perfect choice to head this expedition." Juna boasted of the crafty and audacious burglar to her audience of miscreants. As the blustering crowd cheered the Pistollera's talents and exploits

"As requested, and required, I have fulfilled all particulars of our unwritten contract." Dolores winked at the sultry siblings, throwing back the flirtatious vibe in a none too subtle manner.

The silent Maya leaned forth to drag the haul near, unfastening the straps and quickly probing the contents of each bag. As she nodded to the mouthy, seconds-younger sister, Dolores carefully extracted a velvet bundle from the sling-tote at her hip. Dramatically unfolding the mauve fabric as her eyes kept steeled to her senior counterparts. Revealing the large, gold and green-gemmed cross, the beautiful Catalonian street-orphan turned swashbuckling entrepreneur carefully placed the artisanal relic upon the cloth.

"The prize of Santa Domingo. Quite possibly transcendent of coinage to many a collector."

The room grew silent as everyone's eyes fastened to the perfectly molded crossbars of solid gold, enough wealth to make merchant-princes of every inhabitant within the crowded cellar. Maya picked up the heavy artifact and evaluated it in one hand as the other snapped.

"Havi! Strap her to a foundation block and toss her in the brink."

The giant of a man placed his massive hands on Dolores's shoulders pinning her to the seat as a salty dog tossed a rope upon the table. Remaining calm, Dolores kept her gaze leveled upon the two Spaniards.

"So… I do all the work and you claim the entirety of the reward. Wouldn't agents of the Empire act with a modicum of chivalry… even pirates and thieves conduct themselves with some code of honor."

"We are staking our flag here in Genoa, a valuable acquisition for Castille and Aragon." Juna stated simply, eyes fixated on the holy cross. "With one of your reputes out of our way, we are that much closer to attaining our goals. This town is ours."

Above Dolores's head, a broad-bladed saber slipped deftly under Havi's jaw, the sharpened edge a hair's breadth from his jugular.

"Release the girl or the big bloke breathes blood." A rough, gravelly voice called from behind the strongman.

"I must say, your organization was as easy to infiltrate as the church." As soon as the pressure lifted from her arms, Dolores slipped from the seat to stand out of reach of the large bruiser with the celerity of a mongoose.

Juna set the gold cruciform down to draw a crossbow concealed at her feet as Maya produced a slim dagger and flung it at the Pistollera. Lifting a wooden mug, Dolores managed to trap the airborne blade into the wood, and from there, all Hell broke loose.

Dolores swiped the rope from the table and ran low to the exit as the turbaned man with the saber struck a solid pommel blow to Havi's skull, dropping the big man. Others drew blades of various sorts, and a crossbow bolt flew across the room to plant into the stair rail.

The Purple Pistollera managed a quick knot around the mug's handle as she wove through the mass of men like a serpent winding through bamboo. Prying Maya's throwing knife from the mug, a broken-toothed bouncer tried to clutch her, blocking Dolores's path. With a swift downward thrust of her hand, she sent the blade through the toe of the man's boot, causing him to howl in torment, unable to move his foot. Spinning the cord, she clocked the man under the jaw with the tankard further rendering him inert.

She made her way outside of the hideaway followed by Jerome in Arab garb, Sandro dressed like a pirate, and the speedy Siero. Sandro secured the door with Dolores's rope as Jerome handed her the custom dog lock pistol made specifically for her. With Siero's quick feet taking the lead, the four companions bolted towards the streets.

The hempen cord barrier gave them some distance, but the antagonists from Toledo managed to overcome the obstruction to give chase. Dolores and the Crimson Cinquedeas reached the pulleys and each grabbed hold of a thick rope at various heights. With a practiced chop, Jerome cleaved the counterweight sending the foursome at riveting speed to the building tops. From the safety of the roofs, Dolores turned to gloat at the twins.

"I did my research, Maya and Juna Azaria. No spies and servants for the crown, but criminals and exiles. You should have counted the coins before you betrayed me, for I have already extracted my third of the payment… possibly rounding up in my favor. And good luck pawning off the cross, every authority in the city will be looking for the holy relic seen by thousands of citizens. A theft from the church is a crime with quite high charges."

"Ah, but the crime lies at your feet, Catalonian." Juna glowered up at her rivals, "If the constabulary does not get you first, I shall!"

"I can use makeup not only to beautify, but also to

make myself look older. The Pistollera teased, "I also mentioned on several occasions in disguise that my congregation was sent from Toledo. They will be looking for a middle-aged nun from your homeland. I think you fit the description of the culprit more than I… especially when you bear all evidence. So may the Lord have mercy on you, sisters…for Genoa is far less forgiving."

The Purple Pistollera ended the conversation with a thundering explosion discharged into the heavens from the barrel of her gun. Amidst hoots and laughter, the Crimson Cinquedeas leaped rooftops, vanishing free and triumphant into the Genoese night.

THE MATADOR

Dolores Llorenc, commonly known upon the streets as the Purple Pistollera for the color of her attire and aptitude with firearms, had come a long way since her childhood stay at an orphanage within a convent in Barcelona. Taught the use of the pistol by privateers, learned manners and horsemanship from the French aristocracy, refined her acrobatics amongst the Roma, and graduated her skills of skullduggery and the tricksy arts within the ranks of the Crimson Cinquedeas. Now, the competent and crafty swashbuckler carved her own path in the seaport city of Genoa, besting wits with the powers that be, and aiding the downtrodden and disenfranchised. Her particular set of talents brought the attention of a wide array of employers, seeking her courage and resourcefulness to fulfil an art theft, undergo a rescue mission, or infiltrate the secret recesses of influential personas.

Fra Matteo was one such middleman who often

sought out Dolores's invaluable services for a variety of capers and illicit moonlight adventures. This time, the ex-monk made use of her Spanish heritage, sending her abroad to the capital seat of Madrid, followed by a secondary stop in Lisbon to investigate growing discrepancies along his employer's western trade routes. Since Spain and Portugal claimed the vast majority of the conquered lands of the New World, even the Dark Continent and beyond, the interests that Matteo brokered for, wished to maintain smooth trade alliances with their powerful Iberian neighbors that held Atlantic maritime monopolies with minimal conflict. On the occurrence of such an event, the central powers wished to hold some advantage of surprise and thus, initiative. Matteo, former monk and scholar, ever diligent to the aspirations of his employers attempting to uphold Genoa as the hub that connected the eastern Silk Road from Venice with the ocean ports that sent their large seafaring vessels to the Americas.

Although Dolores was a highly capable and self-sufficient individual of means and attribute, crossing many a field and spectrum of activity, Matteo was loathe to send a lone woman across borders. To his credit, the former monk allowed Dolores to select much of the company that would make the journey with her. Thus, she chose Jerome, jokingly referred to as 'the Moor' by those who willingly or not, misrepresented his exotic features as foreign. His breadth of experience and variety of accomplishments, be they meagre or outright failures, did not dissuade her from wishing her most loyal and honest compadre to journey west with her, the one who guarded over her like an older brother. She procured the others from his Crimson Cinquedea gang; brawny Cleto, the pirate Sandro, since much of the voyage would be by sea, and Giuseppe of Parma for his noble bearing. The small but stalwart contingent of swashbuckling misfits and merry scallywags, accepted with chagrin by Fra Matteo, who made the addition of Alonso the scribe and four guards alongside the crew setting sail upon *La Scorfa Gonfia* across the Ligurian Sea.

The Crimson Cinquedeas chummed well with the sailors, playing games of chance when off duty, drinking, sharing tales and jokes, even taking part in working the riggings by a gang often dubbed feckless freebooters. The guardsmen eventually loosened their regimental bearing to join in on the merriment of the jolly crew. Dolores spent her hours with the navigator and his charts, tried to make the nervous Alonso more comfortable, and quiet, alone time up in the crow's nest – a solitary vigil where she could find distance from the menfolk.

The sailing was smooth as the weather and wind held favorable with the vessel carrying them south and west down the Mediterranean to the ports of Valencia. The band of ten from Genoa made for solid footing off *La Scorfa Gonfia* upon Spanish lands. The merchant ship waved off as the sojourners prepared to ride into the heart of the country.

****

The journey to Toledo was swift and uneventful across temperate lands long tamed and traversed by mankind throughout the millennia. It was here in the City of Three Cultures that the ten foreign emissaries contacted their royal guides, sent to deliver them to the Court of the Hapsburgs. Of course, Jerome spent a pretty penny to purchase a well-crafted blade from the region renown for sharp steel artisanship.

After experiencing a reprieve from travelling half-way across the Sea and Spanish countryside, the odd-ball ensemble followed their escorts north to the throne of the kingdom. The journey to Spain's capital brought about an instantaneous camaraderie despite disparate classes and divisions of heritage of the travelers. None-theless, Dolores felt a growing trepidation at the seat of her bowels worming its way up her spine to gnaw at her brain. The closer they plodded towards their destina-tion, the more the Pistollera dreaded her eventual meet-ing with the emperor that held sway over the grand scope of the globe. Dolores had experienced a fair amount of involvement within high society, but nothing as exalted as the royal courts of a country's monarchs.

Not a soul dare waylay the entourage when guided by a royal escort, and the uneventful journey gave the Catalonian woman an abundance of time to ponder the ins and outs of the various maneuvers upon a chess board where the house held sway and she was granted very few pawns. Thankfully, she retained some dark knights and shadowy bishops in reserve if the need were to arise.

The day came when Madrid's solid fortifications and lofty towers peaked majestically upon the horizon, growing ominously as if the small contingency was ap-proaching to infiltrate the castle…and in a sense, they were. Dolores performed a thorough inventory of her luggage, making sure she was supplied with all effects necessary for palace intrigue, then recalculated all receipts and expenditures with the assistance of Alonso to finalize the discrepancies in finances of their employer. Using a previous alias, Madame Katrina Luiz Montenegro, the half Castilian consort of the merchant-prince Alessandro Peroraro, she insisted her boon companions refer to her as such throughout the remainder of their stay. Drawing one last breath from the open air, she entered the well-guarded gates of Spain's dominion.

****

All ten of the foreign dignitaries, garbed in the apparel of the Genoese merchant house they represented, were well-received by the valet appointed to them and granted rooms outlying the palatial compound. When the newcomers were all well-situated, a steward made his appearance to usher the company to an enclosed courtyard to dine beneath a vine-laced ramada upon the exquisite fare of the nobiliary.

"*Senores, senora*…I am *Senor* Roberto Guadalupe, at your service to accommodate you in whatever we may provide to ensure that your heart is content during your stay in our fair country. Unfortunately, Felipe the Planet King is indisposed with matters of statecraft currently. So, I am here to make sure your experience is enjoyable and satisfactory. In the hopes of fulfilling my esteemed duties, you all have been requested to view our kingdom's long revered bull fights in the most choice of seats. A spectacular display where human finesse is pitted against the brute force and instinctual drive of the ferocious horned beast. Where the barbaric is conquered by the calm training of the skilled Matador…especially once you set eyes upon the undefeated and greatly honored *La Lanza Tierna* in action."

All were enticed by the invitation, even Dolores found herself intrigued by the prospects of witnessing one of Spain's most celebrated sporting events. After receiving unanimous consent, she graciously accepted the invite. The steward excused himself to make preparations and left the emissaries to savor the night's enjoyments.

****

The anticipated day soon arrived, and the ten Genoese sojourners were delivered by carriages to the colosseum that housed the games and orations that entertained the masses. Refurbished from an ancient Roman design, the large staging ring was surrounded by radiating concentric rows, each further arc of seating escalating in height so all could witness the focal point at the center. The party was ushered in to reserved placements with a shaded view of the festivities.

As the colosseum neared maximum capacity, the event was heralded by a band of musicians blaring their trumpets and strumming their stringed instruments. The staccato beat hit a chord upon Dolores's heartstrings, a homage to her land of birth. Reminiscent of her childhood with the fierce flings of the catguts to the claps and stomps of the audience. More driven, more militaristic in flavor then the lilting lows and highs of the Italian melodies. More in line with her hyperactive heartbeat that could keep pace with the quickest.

The musicians circled the arena, their precise notes echoing throughout the stadium until their anthem came to a closure. Lining up along the walled edges of the depressed oval, one of the singers announced the entrance of the first bullfighter before hastily exiting to safer locations. The mood of the crowd shifted noticeably, anticipating the violence about to ensue.

A small, powder keg explosion signaled the beginning of the initial round and a blanketed horse bearing a gaily colored rider holding a small lance aloft, trotted forth. After galloping a couple laps to the fanfare of the onlookers, the picador sent his gelding into mighty leaps and rearing canters. The lancer rode to a resting point at one end of the ring, blowing kisses to the *senoritas* before holding his *pica* on high to signify his readiness for whatever may come.

A dark, ruddy-brown bull was unleashed from behind an iron grate at the opposite end of the picador; confused, manhandled, and enraged. The viewing populace went wild as the combatants faced each other in a battle to determine the fate of both contestants. Behind the rider, red flags draped from the walls of the stadium, fluttered by young attendants attempting to catch the attention and ire of the horned and hooved animal. The equine stirred up dust from the hard-packed earthen floor with its iron-shorn hooves as the befuddled steer became aware of its surroundings. Sighting the manipulated cloths and catching scent of the anxious horse prodding in anticipation, the fledgling bull snorted visibly, instincts perked to danger and aggression.

Taking the initiative, the bull charged, forehead down to gore the taller, thinner animal, tearing across the earth, unstoppable as an avalanche. Knowing full well that to be caught immobilized would be devastating, the picador spurred his steed into motion. The well-trained mount launched forward despite his natural urge to avoid a more furious creature. Galloping into the fray, the horseman dove head-on, then swerved away at the last moment, narrowly missing contact, yet still close enough to allow the rider to pierce the hump behind the broad, horned head of his opponent.

The charge-dodge-stab technique repeated until the enraged and bleeding bull grew savvy to the repetitive maneuvers and trapped the horse from escaping the arc of his curved horns. Backing up onto his hindquarters, the padded steed used his fore hooves as best he could to stave off the pointed cranial protrusions from bowling him over. Desperate to pull out of the precarious situation, the brightly colored lancer broke his spear off into the bull's back, allowing enough distraction to extract himself to safety. Riding away at full speed, the gates opened to allow his departure to the excited roar of the audience.

As the wounded beast attempted, with no success, to extract the barbed staff from its prodded back, a trio of toreros raced out on foot to taunt the bull back into action. The steward explained to the enraptured newcomers that these were the banderilleros, the participants of the middle stage of the fights, entering the arena with acts of extravagant gymnastics from different sides of the *novillo*.

Decked out in outfits of dark burgundy, edged with silver, the three young men entered the ring with cartwheels and backflips performed to aggravate the bull. Turning its head this way and that, the wounded beast ignored his perforated flesh for the oncoming threats. Taking turns distracting the poor, befuddled creature, one of the banderilleros would race in and stab a flag into the thick hide of the shoulders before tumbling away from the thrashing beast with well-honed feats of acrobatics. The brave flagmen managed to get more than a half-dozen fluttering stakes into the bull when the surrounded animal lashed its broad head into one of the annoyances, dragging the man beneath its bulk.

Stomped upon by a fury of hooves, the trapped man's companions rushed in to the save their battered associate from further brutality. One acrobat threw his cape over the bull's eyes, allowing the other to drag their injured partner from beneath the stampeding pounces of six hundred pounds of meat and muscles. Handlers dashed in from the sidelines to keep the bull at bay, giving opportunity for the flagmen to escape. The trampled contestant showed signs of life despite the thrashing received as he was carried towards safety to the great relief of the onlookers.

Dolores peered around at the thousands of viewers, reading their reactions. Many grew squeamish of the violence unleashed upon the banderillero, but more than a few found the torturous treatment of the innocent creature abhorrent. Though she relished in the skills, chutz-pah, and finery of the performers, the torment inflicted upon the unwitting mammal could be called nothing less than cruelty. The mighty bovine was obviously tiring from the numerous punctures that oozed vital lifeblood in thick rivulets down muscular, heaving flesh.

The arena cleared to present the final actor in the third round of the fight. Draped in yellow and gold with a red cape thrown casually over one shoulder entered the matador, bowing formally to the audience. The bull had its head lowered, visibly battered and exhausted, yet enough life seared through its bulk to dive into action as the solar-clothed man shook his bloodred drape. Us-ing the waving fabric to steer the beast, the bullfighter plunged his thin blade into the hefty side of the charger, driving it to the floor, tearing the grip out of the mata-dor's hand. Advancing to the felled creature, he dramat-ically drew the sword from the meaty hinge of the body and ran it straight into the heart, ending the suffering of the wounded giant.

A cacophony echoed around the bowl of the stadi-um for the long and extravagant demise of the *toro*. The matador gesticulated to his adoring public as men rushed in to carry the blanketed carcass away and rake clean any sticky gore from the hard-packed earth. Members of the Crimson Cinquedeas exchanged wagers as the steward addressed Dolores.

"This is not the end, Madame Montenegro. Soon, you will get a chance to see the pride of Spain, Ferdi-nand Adelmo Valentino Salazar, *La Lanza Tierna*."

"The Gentle Spear?" She questioned the title, "Why

would a matador bear such a title?"

Senor Guadalupe handed her a viewing lens, "*Senor* Salazar has never taken the life of any of the beasts he fights, Madame."

"And how does he manage this?" She snorted derisively, "By losing every single battle?"

The steward held a finger to his lips through a slight smile, "Watch Madame, and you shall see…"

Gates were flung outward, and a black, red, and white motley-garbed jester burst into a string of backflips, preceding a new matador garbed in form-fitting red jacket and knickers, sequined in gold emphasizing his broad shoulders and narrow hips. Through the looking glass, Dolores could better make out the odd hat that resembled mouse-ears and his finely chiseled features ornamented with a perfectly manicured moustache and triangular patch of beard that hung from his lower lip. A fine and noble specimen of masculine bearing that any artist would plead on hands and knees to render.

The harlequin continued in his hyperactive antics, somersaulting and springing into the air. The clown was incredibly short, not a dwarf, but barely taller than Dolores who just passed the five-foot mark. When his lithe frame finished the routine, another set of gates flung open to unleash a fresh bull into the fighting field.

The cream white creature was even bigger than the previous bovine, horns narrower, but its physique was brawnier and eyes pink-red and glaring - no young, graduated calf but a full-fledged taurus. Sensing the garish clown in the center of the ring, the huffing behemoth sparked its hooves against the granular flooring. Throwing scarves into the air, the jester set the white bull into motion, initiating the final conflict.

The little patchwork figure cartwheeled out of the way, allowing a clear path for the high-speed duel between horns and *estoca*. *La Lanza Tierna* calmly raised his offhand bearing the billowing cloak of Chinese red silk, catching the attention of the furious animal. With a full circle pirouette, the matador delivered the slightest of pricks just above the back of the left rear hoof. Turning, stirring up the ochre into a cyclone of cascading sediment, the pale stampeder dashed forth on its second pass to settle the score. The wee form of the bell-dangling clown jigged about as the joust resumed.

Dolores's attention was drawn to the fencer's left hand, cleverly held at an odd angle. She realized instantly that he kept something concealed beneath the bright cloth of the cape. *La Lanza Tierna* danced an exquisite improvisation of poise and grace as he spun and dodged to the delight of all watching, his blade, cloak, and the bull a trio of interwoven partners in a tango most deadly. Dolores found herself growing quite heated, unwilling to share the spyglass with Jerome, to his chagrin. The spreading warmth was not sourced from the glaring Spanish sun, but an internal heat that radiated out to the entirety of her body. Doffing her wide-brimmed hat, she fanned herself to soothe the fire inside.

La Lanza Tierna lowered his cape arm and stabbed his sword towards the sky showcasing a dramatic shift in technique. He twirled his cape to and fro as the piebald jester skipped about the ring and the large albino tread forward, dead set on his target. With precision timing, the matador dashed forth to slide beneath the hammering legs as the frisky clown handsprung horizontally from the flank of the rampaging monstrosity.

The white bull came full circle after tearing the cape from *Senor* Salazar's grasp during the overrun, revealing a poignard previously concealed within the drape. Whatever transpired while *La Lanza* dove underneath the bull's vicious charge left the bovine noticeably slowed and unsteady. No visible wounds revealed themselves on the pale, sleek musculature of the horned creature, still, its gait was halted and uncertain. Nonetheless, the enraged beast dragged its hooves across the ground and lunged forth at full momentum.

The patchwork buffoon sacrificed himself for the primary target, leading the racing mass from the slim form of the dual-wielding bladesman. When the chase passed by, *La Lanza Tierna* kept pace, running alongside until the petite clown halted abruptly, spun, and grasped the bull by the horns to be vaulted into the air, flipping to land behind the behemoth on one foot and one knee.

When the albino ceased its thrashing, the matador stood before the enraged hulk. Raising his sword on high, *La Lanza Tierna* brought the ornate pommel down full force onto the bridge of the snout, dropping the bull unconscious. Though the lens, Dolores thought she could make out a slim tear trailing down the dashing figure's face as he knelt to kiss the animal on the brow. Spinning an about face, the grand matador, the pride of the arena, pressed his lips to the hilt of his blade and saluted the audience as the jester tumbled about the course.

Thunderous applause erupted amidst the viewers

graced with the privilege of directly experiencing the greatest sportsman of the land at the height of his performance abilities. Flags, flowers, and even frilly undergarments were thrown towards the center of the stadium as the musicians burst into the ring to blare tunes of victory. Pleased with himself, the steward Roberto turned to Dolores with a broad smile.

"If I read your expression correctly, Madame Montenegro, you seem quite impressed by the day's events. As I said when we met, Espana will not disappoint."

****

Dressed in her finest skirts and corset – black, red, and purple – Dolores coifed her hair before organizing her entourage of rogues and warriors to make sure all were groomed properly and sharply dressed in the colors of House Peroraro. The day had come when the band from Genoa was to be formally introduced to the high court of the Castilian and Aragon alliance. Insisting each enact their roles to the utmost of their abilities, mostly staying silent and keeping their heads low. A rap on the door brought the ensemble to attention as Roberto Guadalupe arrived to usher them into the halls of nobility.

Entering the royal chambers where esteemed guests and official proceedings were hosted in a gaudy, voluminous, and extravagant room designed to house several hundreds of participants to attend to and grovel before the anointed rulers. Directed towards the thrones of King Philip and Queen Elisabeth, a mustachioed man next to a woman with an austere expression lining here heavily creamed face. There was a half dozen men of well-to-do bearing conducting business before the dais that ceased in their affairs to allow for introductions of the new arrivals.

Dolores took the lead, curtsying before the monarchs as her men bowed and kneeled. Jerome groaned, she was not sure if it was caused by his aging knees, or a complete disdain for figures of authority. The Planet King signaled for the guests to arise, and after names were given, he apologized for the delayed hearing.

"I hope you will grant me forgiveness for the late date of our meeting. The heavy burdens of the realm have kept me occupied at every hour, but it would have been most unseemly to have hindered our greetings any longer. I will have you know that I received your Master Alessandro Peroraro's missive some time ago, and I am in full agreement that any discrepancy in trade should be settled immediately, Lady Katrina. In this regard, I have ordered my financiers in to correct the accounts."

Madame Katrina Luiz Montenegro made the acquaintances of the Master of Coin, Cortez Guitavo, a Portuguese trader named Nicolau Bonifacio, and Lorenzo Rinaldi, a Venetian trader also concerned with the Spanish hindrances to the Silk Road. The final member of the financier division, one Levi ben Straussel, was a Jewish banker newly converted to Christianity. At that moment, the guards opened the wide doors revealing the cutting presence of Ferdinand Adelmo Valentino Salazar – *La Lanza Tierna* with his jester companion entering the chamber.

Everyone applauded the matador as he flushed and

bowed to the monarchs. His reds had been swapped out for a similar tight-fitting suit of black and gold with the edition of a dovetail backing to his short jacket. The jester, ever the clown in mask and motley. King Philip rose from his throne to address the bullfighter.

"Bravo, *Senor* Salazar! Though I regret missing your performance, I have been informed in great detail of your ability and bravery within the arena. Come, follow me…I have something for you."

King Philip turned and grabbed a gold medal from the sturdy arm of his seat. Placing the award around the matador's neck, the room burst into another round of clapping and praise. Dolores wanted to devote her attention on the daring swordsman, but duty called, and she had a task at hand.

Various parties formed to mingle, and Dolores sought out the bankers and coin mongers. Throughout her introductions and investigations, she learned that the Venetian Lorenzo was an Eastern silk merchant who had taken the long, overland route across the Pyrenees to reach the heart of Espana. The Portuguese Nicolau was here as an economic envoy for his kingdom to the west, held as a vassal-state by Philip. It seemed that no one trusted the Jew, not for his ethnicity, but for his willingness to convert his religion – a sure sign of betrayal to his community which put into question his loyalty and integrity. But it was the Master of Coin, Cortez Guitavo, who pricked her attention. The weaselly little man with his furtive glances gave her a creepy feeling at the nape of her neck. So, she assigned the scribe, Alonso, to check the books with the shifty financier, while the well-travelled Sandro was sent to befriend the Portuguese. The charismatic Giuseppe would ingratiate himself to Levi the convert, and Jerome, with his Eastern flare, would inquire of Lorenzo why he did not take the more favorable sea journey. Cleto and Peroraro's guards would be on standby if any roadblocks were to arise.

King Philip IV appeared to be in a heated exchange with envoys from the French Bourbons, so Dolores took this opportunity to acquire a glass of aged wine with *La Lanza Tierna*.

"*Hola, Senor* Salazar. I am Madame Katrina Luiz Montenegro. I had the great fortune and pleasure of witnessing your recent display of valor and glory. A truly marvelous engagement unlike anything I have ever beheld. I've seen many a duel and skirmish, yet your chivalrous treatment recalls heroes of yore…a Galahad or El Cid of our times."

The matador blushed again through his olive complexion, "Truly…I confess, I know not how to reply to your praise. I learned my skills from my *papa*. You honor me, Lady." He bowed and they clinked the rims of their glassware together as they absorbed the essences between each other's eyes. "But what has led one as pure and radiant as yourself to need experience such harsh brutality…a merchant's envoy?"

"I am far more traveled and experienced than it may appear, *Senor* Salazar." She fluttered her long, dark lashes up towards the matador. With an unconcealable swell of pride, she added, "I myself have taken part in such endeavors. Yet, like you, I have never taken a life."

The Spanish man swished his beverage between his

narrow cheeks before responding. "If that is so, brave Katrina…than you shall not object to joining me in the Running of the Bulls? Do not fret at the prospects, I will keep you removed from harm."

"Intriguing…though I spent my childhood here, I am not familiar with this ritual." The Pistollera egged him on.

"Then I shall call upon you very soon…you are staying here on the royal grounds?" He stroked the triangular patch of hair below his lip.

"*Si, si.*" Dolores nodded excitedly, "I am housed at the western flank of the palace. Yet, I have my duties here as a representative. I am not on vacation so I cannot enjoy myself fully, unfortunately." She sighed.

"Fear not, beautiful Katrina. I shall devise a plan to sneak you away from the tedium of your occupation, no matter how important it may be." He winked at her with a soft brown eye, "When you visit lovely Espana, you must enjoy the sights…and yourself."

With this final proclamation, their conversation was interrupted by aristocrats congratulating the bullfighter. Displaced, Dolores saw the jester alone in the corner, juggling thin knifes, seemingly bored of talks regarding coinage, or protocol, or obsequious doting. As monarchies of yore, it appeared that the little masked and motley covered man could eschew all rules of decorum. Tired of the menfolk she had traveled with and the banality of court, she approached the acrobatic entertainer.

Noticing the approach of the lovely woman, the clown tossed the three blades in the air, tore his cap from his dark rat-nest mop, and caught the knifes through the tricones of his floppy hat. Grinning wide at Dolores, he redonned his pierced headwear and bowed low.

"Does the gorgeous *senorita* who bats her eyes so adoringly at my cousin wish to speak with little ol' Jerito?"

Her cheeks reddened, wishing she were as coy in romance as she was sly in stealth and subterfuge. She chuckled at the jester's antics as she joked and chatted with the man who stood at eye level with her. Out of nowhere, the wily harlequin cut through the small talk to blurt out a singsong rhyme, eyes rolling in his head.

Heart besotted, Senorita
True identity, incognita
Wagging tongue at mio mia
Pretty little, Kat-a-Rina

The emphasis on her pseudonym made her brows arch – had someone exposed her identity? Or was this long-nosed, pointy-eared jokester hyperaware of all that had transpired? A crisis of faith and purpose raced through her meticulous mind. Sensing an opportunity to better resolve the situation she had been planted in, all the while, unwilling to expose herself further, balancing the risk and reward, which was the tightrope she consistently traversed back and forth, she dared further exposure.

"In your all-knowing wisdom…Jerito, if that is your real name…What should my next course of action be? Since you seem so insightful…"

"Does it look like I am some coin-counter huddled over ledgers and an abacus all day long, Tiny Tart?" The wily rascal mocked her question, "All I can tell you is that in any aristocrat's gilded hovel, things are not as they seem, and a putrescent stank is thinly veiled by a floral perfume. I do declare that my mask reveals a truer face than all present." He finalized his proclamation with a flick to the exaggerated nose of his exquisitely crafted leather half-mask and unleashed a raucous peel of cackling laughter.

****

The Running of the Bulls fell on the Sabbath since it was not technically considered work, rather, a celebration. Ferdinand Adelmo Valentino Salazar sent little Jerito the day before with an invitation for the Lady Katrina Luiz Montenegro to join him at the entry to the event in the early morning. Since it was a day off for everyone, Dolores gathered the Crimson Cinquedeas for a day of merriment, leaving Peroraro's men behind, incase anything were to go amiss.

Despite the enormity of the crowd, mostly garbed in white with red sashes and neckerchiefs, it was easy to spot *La Lanza Tierna* in his matador suit alongside the piebald Jerito, who handed an earthenware jug off to the Cinquedeas with great gusto, obviously drunk at this early hour. *La Lanza* bowed deep and kissed the Madame's hand as she questioned the nature of the day's affairs.

"I am unclear as to our role in this jubilant event. But the anticipation in the air is quite palpable."

"It is good that you wore your knickers and not your flowing gowns, for when you hear the rocket cannon…

run down this road." He pointed down a boarded-up alley, "But for now, we pray."

The prayer for Saint Fermin's protection was given in several languages: Spanish, Latin, Basque. When the benediction came to its finality, a thunderous explosion of black powder set the mob into a frenzy as they all funneled into the alleyway.

She could tell by the gleam in Jerome's eye and jaggedness of his snarl that this type of chaos was his birthright, finally in his element. She trailed just behind the Cinquedeas as they wove through the mass of Spaniards, guffawing and shouldering rushing men out of their ways. Jerito utilized his acrobatic prowess to hop upon windowsills and toe his merry way upon the shoulders of the celebrants.

True to his word, *La Lanza* kept Dolores from being trampled by the crowd of men towering over her. Still unclear as to the reason for the proceeding, Dolores heard a second explosion further adding to her befuddlement and accelerating the swarm of humanity to a greater fervor. From behind, shouts of *Toro Bravo* and screams of excitement and fright roared over the marathon of panting sprinters.

Glancing over her shoulder, Dolores beheld a charging bull, bowling its way through the overcrowded roadway with hoof, heft, and horn, as the agitated cattle cleared his path with a momentum that appeared unstoppable. Realizing, at last, the source of the flight, Dolores screamed a warning to her comrades, praying her message was received. Attempting to pick up pace, but hindered by the speed of those ahead, Dolores, the matador and her crimson covered associates heaved forward, desperate to avoid the goring of the great beast giving chase.

The unavoidable situation came to fruition when the bovine's sparkler-tipped longhorns came into view. Forcing the obstructing participants from his stampede, the bull raged closer to Dolores and her friends. Resigned to the inevitable fact that the corralled and rampaging animal would soon be upon them, the assortment of odd fellows braced themselves for the oncoming threat. Spotting a one-legged beggar propped against a building, oblivious and defenseless to the dangerous rush of the event, Dolores shouted a summons for assistance.

"Jerome! By God, save the cripple!"

Heeding her cry for assistance, Jerome tugged Cleto to his left, hoisting the limb-shorn man out of harm's way. The cacophony grew to a roar as the bull drew ever nearer, tail and horns shooting an array of sparks. Realizing that a confrontation with the large, frothing animal was inevitable, the band of fleeing revelers needed to make lightning quick decisions to avoid a potentially fatal scenario.

Giuseppe, known more for his tongue than his toughness, scaled the brickwork like many of the runners, while Cleto attempted to match muscles with the haff-ton mass which easily threw the strongman aside. Despite his Olympian agility, *Senor* Salazar was bowled flat into the cordoned alley wall by the heaving flank of the insurmountable force of nature. Jerome was slammed, not gored, by the side of a horn, nearly forcing the stubborn ruffian into a coma. Sandro dived to his aid as Dolores stared wide-eyed at the large creature plowing forward, indiscriminate to the destruction left in its wake.

"Duck! Jerito's voice screeched out from behind Dolores. "Kiss the ground, Madame!"

Dolores squatted low with her arms cradling her head as the jester leaped over to clutch the bull by the horns with his scrawny arms. Rearing to its hindlegs, the annoyed bovine launched the little man far behind its rump. As Jerito was catapulted deep into the crowd, Dolores took this opportunity to scurry between the beast's hooves and scramble for safety. The bull continued its charge, leaving the disheveled party behind in its dust-torn tracks. Reassembling their ranks, *La Lanza* lifted Dolores to her feet, panting with desperation in his eyes.

"We must find Jerito! I saw where he landed."

Dolores turned to the Cinquedeas and told them to take care of Jerome with his glazed pupils showing signs of a concussion, then turned to dash after the Matador in search for his partner. Wading through the overcrowded roadway forcing people from his path, Dolores followed diligently behind the swordsman, searching for the little man in motley.

They soon found the unconscious form of Jerito, obviously trampled by the feet of many men. Ferdinand scooped up his cousin from the ground, holding him to his chest like a father cradling a child.

"Come, Dolores. I know where the nearest healer resides."

Racing off to assist the tiny clown, the matador and Pistollera broke through the jumbled citizenry of Madrid to sprint for medical assistance. Reaching the apothecary's hovel, the greying matron answered the fervent pounding upon her door to take in the patient, curmudgeonly and harsh towards the two desperate attendees requesting her help, but tender and doting to the battered and unconscious shell of the jester. As soon as Ferdinand settled his boon companion upon a cot designed to support the injured and infirm, they were shooed off by the elder, determined to aid Jerito, not appreciating an audience hindering her life-saving endeavors.

"…Cracked ribs, but his pulse is strong and feisty. Now get out you two! More will soon arrive today partaking in this foolhardy parade. Macho dunces!"

Exiting the shop cluttered with jars of herbs and vials of ointments, Ferdinand chuckled, "Pay no mind to Lucia's mannerisms, she means well and takes her work very seriously. Jerito should be in good hands." Blushing slightly, he changed the subject, "Would you enjoy some nourishment? I make a fantastic salmorejo dip… if I do say so myself."

Worrying about Jerito and Jerome was trumped by the opportunity to spend an afternoon with this gallant and handsome superstar. Nodding up at the matador, they made their way through the capital, arm in arm. Strolling along the open-air market, purchasing fresh bread, tomatoes, and wine, enjoying the pleasant chats, so different and peaceful compared to the rowdy and dangerous morning with everyone making narrow escapes for their lives. Dolores beamed in the sunlight of this mild summer day, the friendly chatter spoken in her native tongue and affection poured over her by the gracious residents of the city as she shared a pleasant day with a true and gracious gentleman.

The Gentle Spear and the Purple Pistollera meandered their way to Ferdinand's apartment, three-stories up a zigzag flight of iron-railed stairs. Entering the simple, yet elegantly furnished housing, much like her own Genoese rental above *La Tettarella del Drago*, Ferdinand set to task preparing the ingredients for the evening's meal. Dolores, ever ready to jump into action, took her place slicing edibles as *La Lanza* stoked the fire and intuitively combined spices into a bisque most aromatic.

On a worn yet sturdy table, the couple dined upon their home-cooked meal with an exquisite relish that only comes from a well-crafted product resulting from one's own exertions. After a delicious, tongue-titillating experience conjured by an extravagant variety of flavors, Dolores learned of her host's past.

With a mix of modest hesitancy and familial pride, *Senor* Salazar relayed his tutelage under his father, Fredrico, who taught him the intricate art of striking the specific nerves that stun, but do not kill. When questioned about his cousin who saved Dolores earlier in the day, he revealed to the Catalonian how his elder, shorter relative was left stranded upon his mother's death, Papa Salazar took in his spouse's sister's kin. Sharing the hereditary fearlessness, Jerito was trained alongside Ferdinand in the bullring. To stunted to join the ranks of the matadors, the little acrobatic made a perfect banderillero. Wily and wiry, Jerito took on the role of the clown to add his own humor and imprint to his profession.

Dolores was fascinated by the history and mannerisms of her highly skilled and cultivated new friend. Her companions, mission, cares, and woes vanished in the presence of this heroic figure who doted upon her as if she were a Queen. Swooning over this bold yet open and sensitive Adonis was interrupted by a sudden cramp in her heel. Scooting her seat back, she removed her boot to relieve her foot. Ever vigilant, *La Lanza Tierna* knelt to assist the Catalonian in her distress.

"Relax, Madame. As I said before, I am well-tutored in the art of the bodies systems. If you disapprove of my methods, speak and I shall desist."

Massaging the sole of her distressed appendage, the compassionate bullfighter gazed up into the jewels of her eyes, fixated by the magnetism of her daring allure. She curled the arch of her toes seductively, and he took the unspoken invitation to expand the range of his dexterous hands up her shins to knead her smooth and muscular calf. Releasing an involuntary moan, Dolores luxuriated in the careful caresses, no longer bothered by discomforts as her nerves blossomed increasingly towards ecstasy. All boundaries of propriety were shed as he slid up her supine body, spilling from the seat, entangled in a passionate, fervent embrace.

****

Dolores awoke from a romantic evening upon the bedding of Aragon's most revered matador, naked and glistening from the trysting encounter of the night's pleasures. Pleasantly reminiscent, yet coy and shy of the events transpired, she tried to quietly extract herself from the sheets. Despite her aptitude in stealth and secrecy, Ferdinand slowly aroused beside her.

"Mmmm…where are you going, beautiful Katrina?"

She giggled, cupping her exposed breasts, responding to her valiant suitor. "I forgot my duties last night in your tender embraces, dear *La Lanza*." She teased, "I must return to the palace and check in on my cohorts. Especially after the brutal parade we partook in yesterday."

Ferdinand sprung from the bed, bare as a Grecian statue…but more endowed.

"Then I shall escort you. I will not have a lone woman walk the streets of my hometown at the dead of night."

Donning their clothing, the lovers made their way to the palace by moonlight. Sneaking past the gates and guards, the sneaky duo was finally spotted by Jerome, seated upon his room's windowsill with his head bandaged, gulping upon a jug of hops brew.

"Eh…you finally returned, *ragazza*. Glad you remembered those you dragged across the sea to do your dirty work while you frolic with pretty boys and the well-to-do." His sarcasm was as thick as the slur of his tongue.

Jerome dropped from his perch, landing clumsily upon all fours, obviously deep in his cups. Picking himself up from the dirt and dusting off, the rapscallion approached the couple. "It would have been nice if you warned us where you were going. Last I saw you I was nearly speared and trampled. I'm not here to hinder you, but it may be wise to inform us when you disappear on foreign lands."

Hoping to assuage the inebriated and injured man's concerns, the gallant matador approached the Cinquedea. "Fear not, good *senor*. Let me assure you of my guest here…and your friend, that her safety is the highest of my priorities, and, as I have shown, she has been delivered back to her residence whole and sound."

Coming off as a teen attempting to explain to a father why he brought his daughter home at such a late hour, Jerome threw up his hands in exasperation, turning to Dolores and ignoring her suitor. "You come back past the moon and have your abductor speak for you? Spend the night with a man like this and you spread your legs for half of Espana! That's how you get crotch rot!"

Ferdinand would not allow for such a slight and advanced, slapping the drunk across his scarred and bearded face. "Speak to me as you will, but that is no way to talk to a lady!" The matador placed a hand upon the hilt of his blade.

Despite his wounds and weariness, Jerome drew his cinquedea with a practiced hand coiled for alacrity. "Who are you to speak for a girl whose tongue is already well greased? Just another popinjay strutting through life off veneer and finery. Come at me then and see if you can fight something other than cows."

La Lanza Tierna unleashed his much longer, far thinner sword, and with a whiplike flick hit Jerome's armed wrist with the flat of the blade. Jerome dropped his blade and stared open-jawed at his paralyzed hand as the matador socked him square in the side of his face, driving him back to the ground.

Dolores rushed forward, dropping to her fallen friend, getting her body between the two combatants. "Enough of this display, both of you. Jerome may be a drunken lout with a demon's tongue, but I can not have you harming him or yourself. My mission here is extremely sensitive and your boyish antics may draw the attention of the royal guards."

Ferdinand sheathed his sword and bowed low to the Catalonian, "Forgive me, Lady Katrina. I only sought to not have this man besmirch your honor. Don't worry for your friend, he will regain the use of his hand soon enough. I shall depart now, but I pray we have a chance to reunite before you leave Madrid. *Buenos noches, senorita.*"

As the matador slipped away into the night, Dolores clucked her tongue at Jerome, "Your words are going to get you killed one day."

Kneading his hand, regaining the use of his muscles, he picked up his broad-bladed dagger and got to his feet. "Eh…this is the least of my pains suffered throughout the day. Of greater import, while you were off dilly-dallying, some new information has come to light. Our bookish number-pusher, Alonso, learned from Cortez that our Venetian friend has sold all of his goods and departed the city."

Dolores rubbed her temples, pondering the implications of this news. She wrapped her arm around her shaky companion's waist as they headed towards their chambers. "That is intriguing, Jerome. I'm not exactly sure yet how that could pertain to our investigation… but if everything is interconnected, then it may be quite significant. But let us dwell upon it on the morn, my friend. You had quite the rough day and I need you at your best."

****

As the next day's sun disappeared in a rosy-pink hue, five riders stormed towards a wagon, catching their target before it had the opportunity to reach the next town. As the handful of masked equestrians surrounded the transport, the Venetian mercantile team halted their progression, noticeably unnerved by the gang of enclosing highwaymen. Realizing they were ill-prepared to deal with the armed advancement approaching in an intimidating manner, the wagon's guard wisely set his gun to the side in a show of acquiescence.

The rider directly in front of the horse-drawn coach dismounted and drew a firearm. The small figure, cloaked in a black cape and the purple mask of the Pistollera, strolled forward with the barrel of her weapon resting nonchalantly upon her shoulder. She signaled for one of her men to search the contents of the wheeled transport as the three remaining cohorts circled, pointing sharpened steel towards the frightened merchants. When the ransacker extracted a large pouch of coinage from a concealed lockbox, he flipped a Portuguese stamped disc of gold into the free hand of the pistol-wielding spokesperson.

"So, Lorenzo Rinaldi. You not only sought to circumvent Genoa in your greed for riches, but the entire kingdom of Spain." The Purple Pistollera set her sights, quite literally, upon the most elegantly dressed man between the teamsters. "Who was the customer that you sold your Chinese silks for that hefty sum you carry? Answer me true for my shot is aimed directly at your black heart and I have puzzled out enough to know if you lie to me."

The terrified middleman stammered out a desperate response and plea for his life. Satisfied with his answer, she reached into her pocket and flicked a lyra onto his lap to force a fair transaction, whether the sleazy tradesman wished so or not.

"I have a final request for you, fair Lorenzo. Upon your return journey homeward, it would behoove you to visit the house of Alessandro Peroraro and beg forgiveness for sidestepping the customary routes of trade…a monetary penance with further compensation may be in order. Genoa will not be overlooked in global commerce! And I, the Purple Pistollera, will know if my simple invitation is not upheld. Now begone coin-monger, and may our presence be the greatest hindrance on your journey."

The masked woman resaddled and waved her men on. With uproarious hoots and hollers, the band of her rapparee rode back in the direction from whence they came at full gallop.

****

Another day and Dolores dropped the role of the Pistollera for another disguise. In the luxuriant dresses of Lady Katrina Luiz Montenegro, she was summoned to the court of Philip IV for the import of her message. She chose to have Alonso as her sole associate for this meeting, so organizing his ledgers, the scribe accompanied Dolores in all her finery. Along their march through the corridors, they came across the financier, Cortez Guitavo. Urging Alonso to proceed ahead, Dolores engaged the Master of Coin in a private conversation.

"I want to apologize, *Senor* Guitavo. I'll admit, my suspicions regarding the discrepancies throughout the trade routes initially fell upon you, so I had you followed. We did discover your penchant for frequenting orgies and collecting pornographic art. But do not fret, everyone has some issues with the variety of sins the world has to offer, and I am not here to judge. What I am concerned with solely is the realm of finances, and Alonso assured me that you have been fair, honorable, and accurate with all the bills he proofread, and for that, I hope you can continue to interact with me in friendly and noble terms."

Sly and crafty Dolores emphasized the camaraderie while hinting towards insider knowledge that could jeopardize the position of this man of influence, whose shifting eyes revealed his guilt and understanding of a potential threat this diminutive woman could hold over him. Catching up with Alonso at the barrier to the grand hall of the palace through which the three crossed.

The Planetary King was so overjoyed by the appearance of the heroic Catalonian envoy that he sprang from his throne to clutch her nimble fingers, planting devotional kisses upon the back of her hands. "Lady Montenegro, the Spanish Empire is forever indebted to your invaluable services. All you need do is ask and I shall provide what you require."

She retrieved the single Portuguese coin removed from the illicit earnings of the Venetian as Alonso handed over a summary of the tallies that were withheld from both Genoa and Spain. "We were able to extract *Senor* Rinaldi's part in all of this, but he did not work alone." She informed the King as Alonso passed along the starts of a letter. Catching the name at the top of the paper, Philip IV scowled and ordered for ink and quill. Finishing the letter, the ruler rolled up the sheaf and stamped his seal upon it.

"Lady Katrina, I have one final need of your skills. If you will take the road to Lisbon and deliver this to whom the letter was addressed, I shall have a ship prepared for you to take you wherever you desire."

Taking the letter and the King's ambassadorial signet, Dolores decided to make one bold request, "Your majesty, if I may take you up on your offer of generosity, I would greatly appreciate the travelled experience of *La Lanza Tierna* as our guide to Portugal?"

****

Dolores relished the journey west in the company of the Cinquedeas, four Peroraro guards, Alonso, Ferdinand, and his clown cousin, ribs swathed in bandages. The twelve riders made no rush during the final leg of their Spanish incursion, trotting throughout the day and frequenting the inns by evening. The lone female of the group made a game sneaking in and out of the matador's quarters every night.

The beautiful coastal city of Lisbon came into view far too swiftly for Dolores's liking. The ride from Madrid had been amongst the best days of her life – Jerito regaling the companions with comedic pantomimes and an endless array of lore and legends despite his recuperating upon horseback. Dolores was quite amazed that the little jester could make serious Alonso laugh, and the extensive vocabulary with which he told his tales, the almost psychic and prophetic way he could read her motives and next moves absolutely fascinated the Pistollera who found the one figure who could beat her at her own game. She even felt a warmth and slight envy at the easy and open magnetism between Jerome and Jerito. And the dark hours spent in the arms of *Senor* Salazar's secure embrace, an intoxicating blend of exhilaration and pleasant, relaxing contentment.

Onward to business, it was not difficult to find the transgressor of the whole affair with Ferdinand's celebrity and the Cinquedea's propensity for sniffing out a mark. Trailing their target, the crew from Genoa discovered the man consistently frequented a ritzy tavern along the *Rio Tejo* dubbed *O Galo Embriagado* for its cataplana and French wines. It was easy enough for the highly regarded *La Lanza Tierna* to be granted admittance within the establishment alongside his jovial cousin taking the stage, providing levity for the customers as a distraction in the guise of entertainment.

Meanwhile, the Purple Pistollera and Crimson Cinquedeas took advantage of the night to enact their stealthy operations. As the wealthy congregated at *O*

THE PURPLE PISTOLLERA

Galo, Dolores, Jerome, and Sandro crested the rooftop of a small villa. Sandro, the best with lockpicks, was lowered by rope to unlatch a back window before dropping discreetly to the ground to stroll nonchalantly away.

Reeling in the hempen cord, Jerome passed the free end to Dolores for her descent. Her light frame made it possible for Jerome to lower the Pistollera down, hand over hand, tying her off at the unlocked, second story window. Disengaging herself at the sill, Dolores toed her way inside the lavatory.

Exiting the small washroom, the dark clad woman skirt her way past the maids and manservants until she reached the confines of the master bedchambers. Removing a sealed scroll from her bodice, she carefully laid the letter upon a pillow before sneaking her way back the direction from whence she came. Avoiding all obstacles like an impermeable, invisible ghost, Dolores stepped onto the looped end of the harness, tugging upon the rope, signaling her companion to hoist her aloft. From there, two furtive shadows lunged from building to building before scaling down to an uninhabited alleyway to reunite with their fellows in waiting.

To the cunning and conniving Nicolau Boniface,

It has become apparent to your benevolent overlord of your deceitful interactions with the Venetian, Lorenzo Rinaldi, a transaction akin to treachery to King and country. Your paltry and miserly attempts to evade the fair taxations and honest dealings of the customary procedurals of the merchant guilds is a matter of grave con-

cern, a matter of life and death some may argue.

Thankfully for you, I am in the midst of a generous and forgiving disposition, despite your willingness to betray the crown for coin. I suspect a secret patriotism, a longing for the ideal of full sovereignty reclaimed by your own country in opposition to the reality of being a subsidiary state within the greater embrace of the Spanish Empire. Such sentiments could almost be deemed admirable if it were not handled in such an underhanded and self-serving manner.

Regardless, despite my unwillingness to bring the full hammer of the law and justice down upon your now, proven criminality, an example must be made. Henceforth, your ambassadorial title shall be stripped, and a representative of my choosing will arrive to replace you in one month from receiving this missive. Thus, it would be to your advantage to relinquish all illicit profiteering and retire to a locale far removed from any place of sway and connection, in the interest of self-preservation.

- Your Liege Lord, Emperor, & Supreme Ruler, Philip IV the Planet King

On the ports spilling out upon the Atlantic, the entourage from Genoa readied themselves to board the corvette, *A Picada Rapida*. With the menfolk taking care of loading the luggage, Dolores had time for one final private conversation with Ferdinand, the matador.

"There is no way for me to convince you to join our voyage to Genoa?"

The bullfighter looked into her eyes earnestly, as if he could absorb her into the deepest recesses of his mind. "Though I loathe to part with you, dear Lady Katrina, Spain is, and always shall be, my home. I would ask you to stay as well, but your affairs have all been settled and I understand it is imperative that you return. Besides, there is not the appeal for my skills in the lands on which you reside. But your memory will live within me forever more."

Giving the dashing man one last kiss and deep embrace, she whispered her true name into his ear. Jerome approached to draw Dolores from her revery, "The vessel is ready to depart, *ragazza*. We must make the journey home now,"

Ferdinand turned to the man and offered his hand in the spirit of camaraderie. "She is in your hands now, Jerome. Do what you must to keep her safe."

"That is my greatest priority upon this earth." The men grasped forearms in an intimate gesture of acceptance from one warrior to another.

As this transpired, little Jerito popped over to Dolores's side to speak in low tones. "Worry not, O Pistollera. I will keep the bulls from giving *La Lanza* the horn."

Shocked, she turned to the harlequin, "And what makes you so certain I am the mysterious musketeer you speak of?"

"It matters little if I know or not, I now have a tale to tell of direct involvement with the heroine in purple. Some will believe, some will not... that is the nature of stories." The acrobatic, childlike figure skipped away allowing the Genoese no further distractions for making their departure home.

Sails set to catch the breeze; Dolores stood at the rail of the stern watching Lisbon fade into the distance. Jerome approached to console his friend but thought better of it when he heard her crystalline whimpers. Turning away, he kept himself busy cajoling his mates and making introductions with the crew. Dolores was saddened by more than just the loss of love, but at the departure from the beautiful country that birthed her. She unleashed her grief overboard, adding saline tears to the salty sea.

THEFT & THEOPHANY

Climbing down the weathered canyon of the Tomb of Kings was simple as far as descents went, it was the distance that stole the breath from Dolores's lungs. She left her guides above where the rope was secured as she lowered herself, hand by hand, down the sheer cliff, mostly wind-formed with some artificial modifications to the earthen surface.

She met Kareem the Coptic halfway down at a well-concealed tunnel entrance. He motioned her to remain quiet, then retrained his Turkish musket into the torchlit opening. Dolores Llorenc, the fabled Purple Pistollera, adjusted her mask and produced her own dog-lock firearm, taking one last look at the narrow strip of stars to ascertain the hour of the night. Checking the flint and powder, she moved forward, silent in her soft leather shoes as Kareem covered her advancement.

Creeping deeper into the mined hall; her light steps stirred not a speck of dust nor rustled a sound from the loose pebbles she strode gingerly upon. The brief journey through the cavern brought her to a small, window-sized opening high above an eerily lit sanctum, a massive stone block lay flat at the epicenter of the room with ornate bronze torches shedding flickering lights from the corners of the room, held in the arms of animal-headed statues.

The distance to the floor below was at least four times her height, so she gestured for Kareem to retrieve the rope. The hempen cord was swiftly dropped and coiled, before being tossed her way. She fashioned a belay to an iron ring cleated to the hewn wall and clutching tightly, used it to walk down the vertical sides of the chamber covered with hieroglyphs and pictographs carved and painted into the plaster.

Reaching ground, Dolores scanned the array of ancient accoutrements ceremoniously assorted upon the large altar stone. A variety of vessels, crooked wands, a golden ritual dagger, and a pharaonic headdress…the nemyss, iconic symbol of dynastic Egypt.

Her keen senses picked up approaching lights and nearing steps down the room's single corridor, so she scooped up the headwear into her satchel and hastened an ascent. She managed to pull her legs into the tight hole and drag the rope with her as a procession of cultists entered the sanctified chamber. Foreign, undecipherable chants accompanied the pungent aromas of frankincense and fragrant barks burning in urns carried by the ritualists. Dolores, lying flat in her hidey-hole, peered below to witness this occult gathering.

The participants of the ceremony wore large, ornate

masks that covered the entirety of the head and rested upon the shoulders. Lacquered carvings of birds, reptilian representations, and vibrantly colored humanoids with exaggerated features, similar to the torch-bearing idols. Male and female alike left their chests bare, and their lower halves were swathed in smooth kilts of bleached linens.

The formalities of the ritual were initiated with the gong of a reverberating cymbal as the cultists in God-form marched widdershins around the rectangular altar. They each halted at their designated stations throughout the room after one complete circumambulation, consecrating the space of austerity.

One of the priests, mask arching high in the semblance of a long-necked bird, unraveled a scroll of papyrus and began reciting an intonation, voice amplified by the baritone sweep of the resonating headwear.

By Isis, Apophis, and Osiris.

I...A...O...!

L. V. X!

Dolores was taken completely by surprise as an eerie glow burst forth from behind a cross above a carved marble throne, as if by divine grace. Enraptured by the pomp and display of the posture and trappings, she lay rooted to spot with eyes wide and unblinking. She had borne witness to pagan gatherings in the past, but the alien variation of culture held her paralyzed. Nonetheless, the striking similarities with the rituals of the Roman Church, parallel to one of Earth's most ancient civilizations caused a momentary conflict of faith in the thief's breast and brain. The reborn Jesus with its many corresponding overlays to the myth of the resurrected Osiris.

The proceedings continued, centering before the throne at the head of the altar. A blue-skinned figure grabbed the golden athame from the altar and slashed the chest of the one who donned the mask of the dragon. Without flinching, the emulator of the drake snatched the double-honed blade from the aggressor and made a corresponding cut upon his attacker, then kneeled, brandishing the dagger like a knight.

A female approached the mock combatants, flawless in her movements and skin of bronze. Bearing a silver chalice, she gathered the flowing blood from the wounds of both supplicants, set the vessel upon the altar, and began to mummify the cerulean man in lengths of pale cloth. When his torso and limbs were completely bound, he sat upon the throne as she turned back to the altar.

The bare-breasted woman gasped; her following cry of anguish shook all from their mythical reenactments. Scouring every corner of the hallowed chamber, the ibis-headed narrator broke from the chaos to point at the hole where Dolores lay in concealment and shouted with authority to the members of his congregation.

The commotion from the disrupted coven brought Kareem to the fore to protect his charge, unleashing a wild shot from the long barrel of his matchlock, causing a thunderous expulsion as the black powder blast echoed throughout the catacomb like canon fire.

Taking advantage of the sensorial overload, Dolores escaped to the ledge she entered upon and the freshness of the night's air. Realizing she would not have the time needed to scale to her companions above at the rim of the canyon, Dolores made the hasty descent to the ground floor with her faithful bodyguard dogging behind, clumsily handling the rope compared to the lithe Pistollera.

Trusting the sturdiness of her joints, she dropped the rest of the distance while protecting the acquisition cradled in her arms. The stout figure of Kareem trailed behind with far less celerity as Dolores drew her pistol to protect his descent. Since he knew the area far better than Dolores, who hailed from the opposite end of the Mediterranean, he motioned her towards the downgrade as he rammed shot into his spent musket. They bolted through the narrow corridors of the crevice that rent the earth like a scar upon the sands.

Shouts in a language foreign to Dolores's ears were heard and quickly taken up throughout the various portals that littered the rift they sped down. Between quick gulps of air, Dolores questioned Kareem.

"How do we get back to our guides above?"

Panting, Kareem responded through a beard that dripped precious sweat, "Madame, it is of no use…they are men of superstition…and the shouts you heard…the deepest of curses have been called down upon us. They surely have abandoned their station now that the evil eye has been cast upon us."

Dolores's eyes narrowed in disappointment and to keep the rising dust from blurring her vision. "Well… looks like it is just us two then. Stay alive, friend…if you die, I die."

Bolts began to be fired at their fleeing shadows and

the roar of a firearm caused shale from the canyon edge to rain down upon their heads. From ground level cubbyholes, large and swollen men, possibly eunuchs, began to stream forth to pursue the infiltrators. What initially appeared to be a small, esoteric handful of mystics turned out to be a small village of fanatics hot on their trail.

With fresh wind in their lungs, a few of the lighter framed inhabitants managed to close the gap between themselves and the heavyset Kareem and short-limbed Pistollera. One of the pursuers lunged, managing to clutch hold of Kareem's back leg, forcing the Coptic to fall face first into the gravel. Three others dogpiled the tackled man who cried out in shock and desperation. Dolores spun in her tracks and discharged her dog-lock into the air causing two of the aggressors to scramble off her partner and flee back the way they had come.

One of the musclebound brutes was thrown from the struggle as Kareem ferociously wrestled the man who brought him down. Dolores raced to reload her weapon as the disengaged man turned and gave her a backhand slap so forceful, she flew off her feet, landing hard upon the desert floor with her gun spinning out of her grasp.

Her brutalizer stomped over her stunned body, half the size of his own, as he clutched at her throat. The only weapon she had at her disposal was the powder flask she held in her hand, so she unleashed its sulfurous contents into his eyes. Roaring in severe agony, he released her, allowing Dolores to roll out from under him and nimbly spring to her feet.

Seeing Kareem straddled by his attacker, losing the

struggle with the stronger man, she skipped two swift steps and kicked the pointy toe of her shoe firmly into the opponent's ocular cavity, sending the man reeling off her friend. Kareem staggered to his feet and with the butt of his rifle, soundly cracked the skull of his antagonist, then pivoted and proceeded to swing the gunstock at the man trying to clear his eyes, knocking him into an unconscious heap upon the dusty avenue.

Dolores whistled sharply and waved her companion onward as she observed an oncoming horde of torch-bearing predators heading their way. She scooped up her prized firearm and the two companions ran full speed from the advancing mob.

The distance between the top and bottom of the canyon began to narrow drastically, so Dolores took her partner's hand and tugged him into one of several crevices that lined the jagged rift in the landscape. Securing their possessions and weaponry upon their backs, they clambered up the crumbling rock wall to liberty above.

When they reached the point of origin for their mission, Kareem's prognostication was proven correct when they found the camp abandoned by their guides. They praised Providence that their horses and provisions remained. Packing their effects and hiding away the stolen nemyss, they mounted their steeds and rode in the direction of the Nile.

****

Dolores and Kareem waited at the port of Alexandria for the merchant galley, *La Scorfa Gonfia*. The beautiful woman from Catalonia had swapped out her mask and adventurer's attire for the skirts and petticoats of a well-to-do lady. Her dark hair fluttered upon the sea's breeze like a raven flapping its wings as her vessel came into view. Turning to her bearded friend, adorned with his ridiculous red fez, Dolores's voice cracked in open vulnerability.

"In all sincerity, Kareem…I'm nervous to board ship with an item stolen from such a magical land. Especially when under the curse of the evil eye."

The burly Egyptian chuckled and pointed at the silver and pearl rosary that hung from her neck. "No need to fear, Madame, if your faith holds true."

"You say you are also a Christ follower, Kareem. So, tell me…what is a Coptic?" Dolores inquired, nervously stretching and cracking her joints as the merchant ship drew closer.

"We are amongst the first to make a Church for the Savior." He cracked a sly grin at his diminutive friend, "When your Romans destroyed the fragmented Gnostics, we made our way to Africa in order to keep hold to our truth. Our holy books are the oldest and our accounts of the Christ have not been retold and rewritten and on and on but come straight from the source. Yet, I see a pure, if not shaky faith in your gaze. It has allowed you to perform feats that are nearly miraculous, maybe your endeavors will allow you to join the ranks of the Saints, dear Sister."

The ship docked and Dolores held in the tears that would deteriorate the kohl that lined her lids as she reached up to hug Kareem. "I shall miss you so very,

very much, my great friend. You have done so much to help me in this hostile land, if you are ever in Genoa, you will always have a home where I reside."

She kissed the big man's cheek which seemed to steal Kareem's tongue for he was left speechless. Before emotions would turn tide to flood her eyes, she swiveled, grabbed her luggage, and departed the solidity of earth for the uncertainty of the waves.

She was relieved to be leaving this dry and forlorn land with its crocodile-ridden waters and endless stretches of sandy dunes. She longed for the temperate and gentle hills of Europa, with its variety of green-leaved trees that dotted the landscape, to hear voices familiar and understandable. Praying the curse would not follow her, she walked the planks of the ship, bearing her client's ill-gotten gift she had stolen from the Land of the Pharaohs.

SUBMERGED

She plunged, drifting down the azure infinitude like a flake of cascading ash.

Swimming was a skill she never had the opportunity to develop, so she sank through liquescent eternity.

Strange, the pressure of this precious, live-giving substance.

Stagnant breath escapes purpled lips, bubbles bursting before surfacing, as her lungs soon would.

Snaking, smooth scales she could not see, pulling her upwards.

Slowly, to not disrupt the precarious balance, hoisted above serendipitously.

Surface breached, sustaining gasps panted hound-like.

Somehow, she survived, clinging to the remains of her vessel.

Saharan sands or Syrian shores, soon to swallow her like the sea.

JASIAH WITKOFSKY

THE FOUR-CHAMBERED HOOKAH

olores Llorenc stood in the main audience hall of Zazashanade Ty'yl's secret palace, deep within the scorched heart of Arabia. After the disastrous smuggling expedition on the mercantile ship, *La Scorfa Gonfia*, blown to pieces by Barbary corsairs, leaving Dolores washed ashore, lost and alone upon the Levant. Roaming the unknown sands, bleached and ochre, the stranded foreigner plunged deeper into the desert in search of civilization.

It was upon the dunes of the Fertile Crescent that Dolores encountered a small caravan of camels and horsemen. The lead Muslim rode her down and tackled the small woman, roping her arms and trailing her behind his mount. As the men halted their trek to set up camp for the evening, the crafty lady extracted a thin blade she kept concealed within her corset. Severing her bonds as the men cooked over braziers, Dolores took the opportunity to sprint to the horse that still bore her satchel. Whipping the steed to a frothing gallop, she shocked the pursuing Arabs with her riding prowess. Providence was on her side, for she had stolen the swiftest stallion and soon left her captors far behind her dust trail.

She rode on beneath the stars that shone as furiously as they did upon the seas. When she came upon the first sign of vegetation: some thorny shrubs and a tiny copse of date palms, she finally allowed herself to halt and rest. When she woke, she was thankful for the large brim of her cavalier's hat that kept the harsh sun from blistering her flesh. She had no means to cook the pilaf grains she found in the saddlebags, and the exotic spices seared her tongue, so she carried on, straining her eyes for any sign of life or hospitality.

Affairs continued as such for another day with Dolores finding her goatskin emptied of its precious liquid content. The dark-maned stallion had grown so weak, Dolores was forced to dismount and lead the Arabian north and east. When dusk arrived to lessen the severity of the desert's heat, the setting crimson sun revealed four minarets jutting from the imprint of a gigantic depression. Descending the dunes, Dolores stumbled upon a low palace cornered by the towers, the same tawny color as the sands, with pastel highlights still visible in the fading light. She barely had the strength to drag the captured stallion to the entry where she promptly fell unconscious before the citadel's doors.

Dolores arose upon silks and satins, attended to by beautiful, dusky woman who slowly filled her parched throat with sweet water infused with herbal extracts. When the hollow pit of Dolores's stomach became audible, the caretakers giggled and fed her falafel garnished with mildly curried lamb cubes. The starved woman from Catalonia was so famished, she gulped the decadent meal down, believing each bite to be the most delicious experience of her existence.

When it was determined that Dolores was suitably recovered, the attendants bathed the petite Spaniard in perfumed waters. They swathed her athletic nakedness in silks of sheer pinks, oranges, and reds. Donning the customary veil that covered the lower half of the face, Dolores was ushered forward to be greeted by the Lord of the sanctuary that had sponsored her recuperation.

****

Dolores stood in the antechamber with four bald and massive eunuchs in each corner, armed with broad falchions and brass-inlaid muskets. Despite the surprising coolness of the room, Dolores found herself sweating beneath the nearly transparent sashes that draped her body.

The duration of Dolores's wait seemed endless, standing poised in the middle of the large chamber, until the embroidered curtain before her was raised, revealing a similarly garbed woman lounging upon a heavily carpeted dais. The dark, exotic beauty had ebony ringlets that spiraled down her back to cascade upon the pillows that supported her delicate frame. The black curls contrasted sharply with the painted, almond-shaped lids that contained her penetrating sea-blue eyes. She turned her piercing gaze from Dolores's firearm, which lay before her, to the owner.

"Marhabana sayidati."

When the lady of the house saw the confusion written upon Dolores's face, she changed both tactics and language.

"This is a most exquisite contraption, Madame…"

"Dolores…Dolores Llorenc." The guest gave a curtsy as she responded to her host's perfect Spanish.

"I hope you do not find it too intrusive, but I must be extremely attentive about everyone and everything that enters my palace." The lounging woman patted an embroidered throw-pillow, urging Dolores to take a seat beside her, handing the pistol back to its owner. "Welcome to my castle, Madame Llorenc. I am Zazashanade…you can call me Zascha, and everything within my lands is at your disposal as long as you are my esteemed guest."

The two women dined upon dried fruits and fine wine as Zazashanade asked Dolores to regale her with a tale. The European told of her Catalonian upbringing and Italian escapades, as the lady of the palace edged ever nearer. The biography was concluded with the shipwreck, leaving out the purpose of her secret mission, leading to the desert journey which led Dolores to where she sat currently. Yet, curiosity got the better of Dolores, as it often did, and it was her turn to probe her host.

"Lady Zascha, I do not wish to breach propriety, but how is it that you, a lone woman, have come to rule an entire palatial residence in the heart of Muslim lands, where the menfolk hold absolute dominion?"

Zazashanade halted her smooth caresses of Dolores's exposed shins as she tilted her head back, laughing with gusto towards the heavens. "Oh, sweet Dolores. Mohammed walked these lands less than a thousand years ago. My tradition is far older. I am a Zoroastrian, descending from an ancient lineage of Magi. I take my counsel from the Genies, bound spirits of immense power and immortal genius."

Now, it was Dolores's turn to chortle in disbelief at the preposterous claims. Zazashanade arced her delicate brows in consternation as she snapped one of her castrated warriors to attention. In their native tongue, Zazashanade sent the eunuch to another room. He swiftly returned, cradling a bizarre contraption of copper and glass orbs which he gingerly placed between the two women. With a flourish of her henna-painted hand, she dismissed the guards, leaving the females alone to their private affairs.

Zazashanade sprinkled a powdered, herbal mixture atop the strange, multichambered vessel, bedecked in various elemental sigils, as Dolores watched in bewilderment. The entrancing Arabian woman lit the pungent concoction from a brazier, igniting the aromatic bouquet while inhaling the smoke through one of four tubes that protruded from the alembic device. She handed her guest a juxtaposed nozzle and gently coaxed Dolores to imbibe of the billowing vapors.

"Yes! The Djinni, the Efreeti, they lend me their knowledge…and so much more…"

Dolores hesitantly received the inhalation apparatus, unsure whether participation would forever devastate her consciousness, and how rude it would be to refuse. Jerome and his band of Crimson Cinquedeas

continuously offered the pipe, filled with foreign tobacco and eastern hashish, a combination so harsh and rank
it made her virgin nostrils recoil in disgust. Regardless,
the blend she was now offered smelled both enticing and
delectable. Zazashanade ensured her it was a carefully
measured amount of Persian poppy and Tibetan herbs,
so Dolores decided to make herself vulnerable to this
novel experience.

Breathing in the alchemic mystery, Dolores sput-
tered and snorted blue-green smoke like a fuming dragon. She coughed out the contents of her lungs as she
fell back upon the hand-woven rugs. Through a haze
of smoke and blurred visualizations, Dolores made out
a ritualistic, singsong chant from Zazashanade's painted lips as the smokes began to coalesce, taking shape…
taking form.

****

Dolores was brought back into her body by
Zazashanade straddling her supine figure, lightly kissing
her revealed skin. Hovering above the Arabian beauty
was a large, voluptuous female form, molded entirely of
crystal-clear water. Her dark, lustrous hair swayed like
kelp strands as her deep, azure eyes gazed upon the erot-
ic coupling with a primal and undisguised lust.

Dolores succumbed to Zazashanade's caresses, exposing her paramour's breasts for her hungry mouth. As
all clothing was stripped from smooth flesh, the liquescent outline of the elemental being dissolved, completely engulfing the lovers. Submerged in the warm, froth-

ing waters, Dolores was amazed to find that she could still breathe as she returned her suitor's passionate kisses. Afloat amidst the sensuous pool, the two intertwined women danced in an embrace of bubbling, aquatic ecstasy.

****

Dolores awoke, rising naked from the cushions and silks that engulfed her. She quickly pulled her loose clothing over her blushing figure as she realized Zazashanade was in deep conversation with an elderly man. The turbaned and pantalooned being floated cross-legged above the ground and his skin was nearly translucent. When he turned his spectacled gaze upon Dolores, Zazashanade halted her resinous inhalations from the waterpipe to introduce the two.

"Madame Llorenc, this is Kabushkan. My Vizier and wisest of advisors."

The clear-skinned man bowed at the torso, "Lady, it is a great honor to be graced with your esteemed presence."

The otherworldly man politely turned back to his philosophical musings, allowing an exposed Dolores to garb herself properly. The hovering elder was playing a game of chess with the lady of the palace as they debated epistemology. When Dolores cinched together the last of her sashes, she reclined beside Zazashanade to nibble skewered meats while perking her ears towards their conversation.

"But Kabushkan, if the Gods are truly responsible

for the creation of life and all of the cosmos, can we truly claim to be the originator of our own thoughts and actions? How can we be the creator when we ourselves were created?" Without a glance, Zazashanade handed her newfound friend and lover a hose from the smoldering hookah.

"My dear Lady Zazashanade, in my centuries of experience, I have found that you always have a choice. Even I, bound to your precious smoking device, can still decide how I shall handle my captivity. I share this prison, no offense my beautiful captor, with the other djinni, and we all have a choice on how we decide to handle our circumstances. The more internally you reside, the deeper you travel within the realm of the self, the more you shall discover that self-determination is the hallmark of the individual." Kabushkan stroked his white, zig-zag beard as he turned his attention to the foreigner. "And what say you dear guest of my august and illustrious lady? Does, fate, fortune, or free-will dictate your endeavors?"

Dolores waded through the heady vapors that sought to cloud her vision and dull the edge of her razor-sharp mind. This interaction brought recollections of dialogues with her friend Jerome, who was more philosophical than religious. Clearing her parched throat, she responded to the ancient entity that floated before her.

"Back in my home of Genoa, I would often argue with my greatest compadre over subjects both petty and monumental. When he, Jerome, is deep in his cups, which is often, he typically falls into dark moods. During these spells, I try to snap him out of his fatalistic out-look. He always counters that it is his sole determination which drives his gloomy disposition…a clear view of a dark world. He consistently, stubbornly, insists upon this point. So, I suggest that life is a combination of all three of these concepts. Providence, chance, and in-dependence together play a part in God's machinations. For there are factors beyond our control that precede us, and yet, the Almighty has granted us decisive power to respond to such occurrences, as your Vizier suggests. If choice was everything, I would like to have known my parents and saved those things I held dear and lost. Yet, I have managed to carve my way through this world… to some extent."

Kabushkan nodded in approval, impressed with the Catalonian's answer as he stroked his lightning bolt goa-tee, as wispy as the clouds. "Well Lady Zazashanade, it appears that you have found a woman of such inge-nuity, that it is no wonder she was able to discover your discreetly obfuscated fortress. Well spoken, Madame." The spectral entity bowed once more towards the new-comer.

"A matter of kismet my Vizier." Zazashanade spoke before pulling Dolores closer to savor her lips yet again.

With a resigned sigh, Kabushkan forfeit his bish-op to place his opponent in an inevitable checkmate. "Well…it seems our conversation has finished, just as our game has concluded. If you have no further need of my services, you know where to find me."

The two women, so enthralled by each other's ro-mantic embraces, were oblivious to the djinn dispersing into the heady atmosphere.

****

Dolores peeled her heavy lids apart to find Zazashanade arguing with a child of flickering flame before a map of the region. The youth's body was surmounted by a topknot of torchlight that whipped about furiously as she lectured the queen of the harem with gusts of dense smoke punctuating each of her exclamations.

"Your accepting nature has gotten the best of you, Zascha!" The fiery Efreeti hissed. "If you keep allowing the ever-expanding Mohammedans into your lands, then they shall override your bastion, and all shall be lost!"

Zazashanade queried, "And what should I do, Jahnni? Eradicate any Bedouin that verges anywhere near our safehouse? With a handful of eunuchs and a small group of disparate Djinn…unlikely at best."

While the flaming girl argued with the ruler of the seraglio, Dolores dared to raise her head from the fragrant cushions. Her addled movements attracted the attention and ire of the fire child, who sent her ember stare burning into the heart of the unsuspecting Spaniard with a ferocity of erupting lava. Turning away in disgust, the igneous whelp shrieked at her mistress.

"Curse you Zascha! It is one thing to bring your playthings to your bedchambers, but you have allowed a foreign infidel into our war counsel! I should incinerate her where she lies!"

Zazashanade stood abruptly and threw out a commanding proclamation. "No Jahnni! I order you to perform no harm upon my guest!"

"As you wish Lady." And with that, the flame-red youth turned and blew a terrific plume of noxious smoke, completely encapsulating Dolores. The unsuspecting Pistollera coughed and wheezed as she attempted desperately to draw a breath devoid of ash and cinder. Unable to procure sufficient, life-sustaining oxygen, Dolores fell over in a swoon, swifter and more deeply than the narcotics of which she had recently imbibed.

****

Dolores pierced the haze of unconsciousness to find herself cradled in the firm arms of a rocky behemoth with green fronds for hair and thick, mossy brows. His bedrock biceps and granite pectorals held the bedazzled heroine safe as his lower half carved a swath across the sand and gravel terrain.

Even though she feared this stony monstrosity who was transporting her to some unknown destination, she clung to his hardened physique with a desperation born of a lifetime of piqued survival instincts. Her whipping hair and the billowing desert sands blurred Dolores's vision to the point of blindness. So, she held tight to this earthen figure, as helpless as a babe.

When the statuesque creature noticed that his passenger stirred, he stared down at her cold and stoic, tightening his hold on her, shielding her from the stirring dust storm his whirlwind gyrations tore from the dunes.

Dolores Llorenc awoke upon a small, yet verdant oasis, clothed in her Western attire with the black stallion lapping clear water from a nearby pond. Trying to recall every detail from the narcotic-fueled revelry of the past couple of days, she could not ascertain whether her recollections were real, psychotropic hallucinations, or a very vivid dream.

She made an inventory of her satchel and saddlebags, discovering that her rations had been replenished and her pistol and dagger safely tucked away. A scroll rolled out of the last carryall, which she unraveled to reveal a map directing her northwest back to Europe…one piece of evidence that she had indeed met a friend within this hostile environment.

Splashing moderately cool water upon her face and arms, Dolores mounted her stolen stead and followed the map's guidance along the arduous trek back home.

ABOUT THE AUTHOR

The antivillain known as Jasiah Witkofsky is an independent author, editor, philosopher-gardener, artistic dabbler, rock n' roller, and rabblerouser dwelling amidst the majestic Sierra Nevadas of Northern California. His works can be found on both hemispheres of the globe, three continents, from several anthology companies.